GLOBAL WARMING

A WEAPON OF MASS DESTRUCTION

I0679638

A Novel By

G S WILLMOTT

ACKNOWLEDGEMENTS

Preview Readers

Martin Humphreys

Ian Jones

Tony Pittard

Cenred Harmsworth

Anna Shearer my wife for putting up with me.

CONTENTS

NAVAL AVIATOR

THE BEST JOB IN THE WORLD

CHAPTER 1

November 1966

Newport USA

Mathew Ericson was sitting at the dining table with his wife Janine and their two children; twelve-year-old Jacob and Mary, who was ten. It would be the last meal they would enjoy together for some time. Mathew was a navy pilot attached to the aircraft carrier *USS Ticonderoga*.

He would be leaving the following morning. *USS Ticonderoga* would be joining several other ships off the coast of South Vietnam as the war had escalated.

'I don't understand why we are getting involved in the Vietnam War Dad,' Jacob said.

'Well, son, America doesn't want South Vietnam to be invaded by the communist north. If she falls then there will be a domino effect. Laos, Cambodia, Burma and Thailand could become communist. If all of Asia becomes communist we could see World War III.'

'Why is communism such a bad thing, Dad?' asked Mary.

'Communism is an oppressive form of government, Mary. Joseph Stalin, the Premier of Russia, killed over sixty million of his own people. Stalin's famous quote was *'A single death is a tragedy; a million deaths is a statistic.'*

'Well, China's a communist country and we never hear anything bad about them.'

'That's a good point, but they are a closed country with one billion citizens and they are very secretive apart from blowing their trumpet when they exploded their first nuclear bomb a few weeks ago.'

'Our Government believes the "Cultural Revolution" Mao has started will eliminate millions of Chinese people.'

'It's also believed they are helping the North Vietnamese.'

'I think that's enough about war and communism. We should be enjoying our last meal together,' said Janine.

'You're right darling; enough of that.'

The family finished their dessert and went into the lounge room to watch *Bonanza*.

When Bonanza finished the children went to bed, as did Janine and Mathew.

'I think we should have a bit of a play, darling, since you're going away for who knows how long,' said Janine.

'That's an invitation I can't refuse, my love. Come over here and take that nightie off.'

The married couple made love not once but twice. They both then settled into a sound sleep.

The alarm woke Mathew at 5.30 am. He got out of bed, showered, and dressed in his naval uniform. He looked at himself in the long mirror. He loved to see himself in uniform with the three gold stripes on his cuff. It made him feel important.

Janine got out of bed and donned her robe. She sat at the kitchen table with her husband, drinking coffee.

'You be careful, darling, flying that damn fast plane of yours.'

'Don't worry, I'll be extra careful. I'll be coming home to my family unharmed.'

'All right. Well, you better get going; it's seven o'clock and you don't want to miss your ship.'

'No, I'll just look in on the kids before I go.'

Mathew sneaked into Jacob's room. He was still fast asleep. He kissed his son on the cheek, and did the same to Mary.

Janine gave her husband one last hug at the front door and waved to him as he got into the taxi.

It was a short cab ride to the Norfolk Naval Base. As Mathew approached the base he was once again in awe of the size of the facility.

Naval Station (NS) Norfolk, the world's biggest naval base, is situated in south-eastern Virginia in the Sewell's Point peninsula of Norfolk city. The base was established in 1917 and covers an area of approximately 3,400 acres.

Norfolk Navy Base

The taxi cleared the checkpoint and drove to the end of the dock where *USS Ticonderoga* was moored.

He walked up the gangplank and made his way to his cabin, which felt like his home away from home. This was his eighth tour of duty flying jet fighters from *Ticonderoga*'s flight deck. Once Mathew unpacked his bag he made his way to the Airwing Commander's office.

Gordon Taylor had been in the Airwing of the United States Navy since leaving college with a Degree in Mechanical Engineering. He and Alistair Bingham, the ship's commanding officer, were of an equal rank in the chain of command.

'Good morning, sir.'

'Oh good morning, Mathew, it's good to have you back. Did you enjoy your break with the family?'

'Yes, sir, very much so.'

'Well, we've got some real work ahead of us this time. No more war games; this will be the real thing.'

'Yes, sir I'm well aware of the situation and I'm ready to do my best.'

'I'll see you in the officers' mess for dinner.'

'Yes, sir.'

Mathew saluted his superior officer and made his way down to the hanger bay to inspect his aircraft.

Although the hangar bay on the *Ticonderoga* aircraft carrier was large, it wasn't large enough to store all the aircraft.

To overcome the problem, the planes were securely tied down with chains that attached between tie-downs on the deck, and attaching points on the aircraft. The heavier the expected weather, the more chains were used to secure the plane.

Mathew walked through the bay until he found his trusty Skyhawk Fighter. He would be flying sorties over Vietnam in this plane; the first time he had flown in a war zone. One of his responsibilities as a senior pilot was to always carry two B43 nuclear bombs. He hoped he would never receive the order to release them.

Once the ship's 5000 crew were ready, the magnificent *Ticonderoga* was escorted out of the bay by three tugs. She was released when the carrier reached the mouth of the estuary. The tugs returned to base, having done their job once again.

The voyage was going to plan; the pilots refined their skills by flying sorties over the Pacific Ocean, the food prepared in the galley was excellent and the movies shown were second to none. The movies the sailors and airmen were watching were the same as the folks back in the States saw. Popular were *The Sons of Katie Elder, The Cincinnati Kid, The Great Race* and *Battle of the Bulge*.

After sailing for thirty days *Ticonderoga* was close to the Fijian Islands.

December 5

The day began like any other day on board *Ticonderoga*; Mathew ate a hearty breakfast of bacon and eggs with hash browns on the side and a mug of black coffee.

He was due to take off at 10 am. He went down to his cabin and put on his flight suit. His helmet was already waiting for him in the plane.

He caught the lift down to the hanger bay and boarded his plane where he began his pre-flight check while waiting to be manoeuvred onto the plane elevator, which would take him up two decks to the flight deck.

Plane Elevator

The crew indicated to Mathew that they were about to roll the Skyhawk onto the elevator and he gave them the thumbs up.

No one was sure what happened to cause the accident, but Mathew in his Skyhawk fell over the side and sank in 14,000 feet of water. Mathew, the plane and the two nuclear bombs were never recovered.

It was Gordon Taylor, the airwing commander's, sad duty to inform Janine of Mathew's death.

SUCCESS

IS WHERE PREPARATION AND OPPORTUNITY MEET

Bobby Unser

CHAPTER 2

Richard Manson was sitting at his walnut art deco desk. It was one of his prized possessions, having been designed by Frank Fletcher and manufactured by Fletcher Aviation in Pasadena, California.

Frank Fletcher had much more success in designing and manufacturing furniture than he did with aircraft.

Richard was an accomplished aviator who served as a fighter pilot during the Vietnam War. Richard had two great passions, aircraft and art deco design, whether it be furniture of buildings.

He owned examples of both. He was the proud owner of six aircraft and he also possessed an art deco building.

The Manson Tower was built in the 1930s in the art deco style. It boasted forty-three storeys and was located at the prime address of 275 Madison Avenue in midtown New York.

How did Richard Manson go from being a fighter pilot to being one of the richest men in America?

He attended Stanford University in California once he returned from Vietnam, studying electrical engineering. He was dux of his final year and his professors encouraged him to continue studying for a Masters' Degree. He declined, as he wanted to enter the workforce and earn some money. Several companies were keen to offer him a position but he eventually accepted a job at Honeywell. Richard moved to New Jersey to take up his new role with one of the largest electronics companies in the world.

His time at Honeywell was challenging but enjoyable, and spent in designing circuit boards for the mainframe computer division.

It was at this time that Richard began tinkering with design concepts at home. He also taught himself how to program.

After two years he had designed a personal computer and an operating system.

IBM had recently released the PC using Microsoft's operating system DOS.

The young inventor called his computer the IMP, an acronym for Intelligent Micro Processor. The major advantage the IMP had over its competitors, IBM and Apple, was its operating system was menu driven and could accommodate sixteen users.

He began selling his computer through specialist magazines and it didn't take long for word to get around amongst the computer geek community.

The IMP went viral. Richard outsourced the manufacturing process to a small New Jersey-based company called Hewlett Packard.

After two years on the market he received an offer from a large computer company to buy the company. After significant negotiation he accepted $10,000,000 as a fair and reasonable price.

Richard decided he should invest in real estate so he bought a restaurant site in Queens. He had no sooner settled than McDonald's made him an offer he walked away with a $100,000 profit.

Over the following ten years, the young entrepreneur bought and sold several New York buildings. His largest investment was 275 Madison Avenue, which he renamed Manson Tower.

Other investments were several start-up Silicon Valley companies. Not all were successful, but most of them were, particularly Apple.

He purchased several golf resorts around the country and a New York hotel.

By 2018 Richard's estimated worth by Forbes was $50 Billion.

He had always had a fascination with lost treasure in the oceans of the world, probably a boyhood fantasy. The advantage of being a billionaire is you can bring your fantasies to life.

Richard purchased a ship from a treasure hunter, Mal Fisher, who was retiring due to ill health.

Richard renamed the vessel *Aurarius* which meant gold digger in Latin.

The ship was well equipped with sonar and a very special piece of equipment; an unmanned deep-towed undersea video camera sled developed by Dr Robert Ballard. This piece of sophisticated equipment was instrumental in discovering the wrecks of *Titanic* and the *Bismarck*.

He christened her the *Sea IMP*.

A crane was also installed at the stern of the ship for lifting heavy objects, such as crates of gold, off the ocean floor.

Sea IMP

The ship had a crew of eight plus six deep-sea specialist divers. Overall, *Aurarius* was a very well manned and equipped salvage ship.

Aurarius was on a very important mission in the South Pacific. They were searching for a merchant ship, *SS Vanderbilt*, that had been sunk by a Japanese submarine in 1943 close to the Fijian archipelago. The reason Richard had shown interest in the wreck was that the *Vanderbilt* was en route to Australia with $ 1,000,000,000 in gold bullion on board. It was a gift from the US Government to help Australia remain a fortress from Japanese invasion. The money was to be used for aircraft and a large radar shield near Darwin in the Northern Territory.

The value of the bullion when *Aurarius* set off on its journey was estimated to be $14, 000,000,000

Aurarius left its berth in San Francisco on 12 May. It would take eighty-five days at sea before reaching Fiji; a considerable amount of time for the crew and divers to be confined on a ship.

Richard was planning to join the ship once it reached the search area. He would fly from New York to Sydney then catch a flight to Nadi in Fiji. He would then rendezvous with *Aurarius* via helicopter, landing on the ship's helipad.

June 30

The skipper of *Aurarius* was Stewart Fairweather. He had salt water running through his veins. He had enlisted in the United States Navy at the age of seventeen and served for twenty years before accepting an honourable discharge with the rank of Captain.

He had been in command of *Aurarius* for three years.

Captain Fairweather was standing on the bridge. The seas were calm, and there was a gentle northwest wind blowing. It was conditions like these that made his job so enjoyable.

Something caught his eye on the horizon; a low white cloud in the distance, moving towards them at a rapid speed. He knew immediately what it was, a white squall, a storm so powerful it could capsize *Aurarius*.

He alerted the crew via the ship's communication system, ordering them ensure all equipment on the deck was secured. The *Sea IMP* was the most valuable piece of equipment; therefore, two of the crew added extra ropes to tie her down.

When the white squall hit the ship, the wind speeds were estimated at 140 kilometres an hour. Tarpaulins were being ripped off and disappearing overboard. The ship was bobbing about like a child's toy, and waves were breaking over the sides. Captain Fairweather was finding it difficult to keep the ship on course.

Aurarius began to list to starboard. Things that had been tied down went over the side, including several dive tanks. As quickly as the white squall was upon them, she disappeared. A calm ensued over the ship. The crew were walking around in a daze, not sure what to do. The captain ordered all men on deck to check what had been lost in the storm. The losses were light; five dive cylinders and a water pump. The most important piece of equipment was still firmly tied; the *Sea IMP*.

White Squall Approaching *Aurarius*

Fairweather used his satellite phone to call Richard and inform him of the storm and the losses.

'Hello, Richard, it's Stewart. We have just encountered a white squall and things got pretty rough for a while.'

'My God, is everyone okay?'

'Yes, no injuries, but we lost some equipment.'

'Equipment can be replaced, but is *IMP* okay?'

'Yes, she's fine. We tied some extra ropes on her just before the squall hit.'

'So, Stewart, what do you need from me?'

'We lost five dive cylinders and a water pump.'

'I'll bring them with me when we meet up in a few weeks.'

'Thanks, Richard. As you no doubt know, we are on schedule and we should reach Fiji by the first week of August.'

'Excellent. I'll see you then. I hope you don't encounter any more inclement weather.'

'So do I, Richard. Goodbye.'

ANOTHER DAY
ANOTHER COUP

CHAPTER 3

Fiji has not had a stable government since winning independence from Great Britain.

A summary of the turmoil:

1970 - Fiji wins Independence after a century of British rule.

1987 - The first of two coups overthrow the Indian majority government of the elected Prime Minister, Timoci Bavadra.

1999 - Mahendra Chaudhry is elected Fiji's first ethnic Indian Prime Minister. Exactly one year later, on May 19, 2000, he and most of his cabinet are taken hostage by coup leader George Speight. The Fijian President Ratu Sir Kamisese Mara in turn sacks Speight's government on the basis they are unable to exercise their duties. Mara's intention is to assume emergency powers and govern in his own right.

However, Commodore Frank Bainimaram disposes him.

2014 - Former military leader Frank Daurewa is elected Prime Minister, eight years after seizing power in a coup.

Fiji is an island nation in the South Pacific. The country is made up of over 300 islands, of which 110 are inhabited. The two main Fijian Islands, Viti Levu and Vanua Levu, account for 87% of the population of almost 850,000.

The capital of Fiji is Suva, situated on Viti Levu. Almost three-quarters of the total population live in Suva.

Important towns are Nadi, which is the location of the international airport, and Lautoka, which is a large seaport.

Other important islands in Fiji include Kadavu Island, the Lau Group, the Mamanuca Islands and the Yasawa Islands. The majority of Fiji's islands were formed through volcanic activity. There is still some geothermal activity today on the islands of Vanua Levu and Tavenui.

Because of the abundance of forest, mineral and fishing resources, Fiji is one of the most developed economies in the Pacific island realm today. Natural resources include timber, fish, gold, copper and offshore oil and hydropower.

Fiji also has a significant amount of tourism with many people choosing Nadi or Denarau as their preferred destination. The biggest source of international visitors comes from Australia, New Zealand and the USA.

The soft coral reefs of Fiji are the main attraction but there are also many other activities for people to enjoy such as fishing, surfing and jet skiing.

Mel Gibson purchased his own Fijian island for $17,000,000 and Nicole Kidman has owned a luxurious holiday home on another island for some time.

The Fijian people were concerned about the effect climate change was having on their island paradise. The government, however, were regarded as global warming sceptics.

Prime Minister Daurewa had just dictated a letter to the United Nations rejecting their offer for Fiji to act as President at the upcoming climate change conference to be held in Bonn, Germany. He decided to send a representative but that was as far as he would go.

The former Fijian Government had accepted the UN report the previous year.

Change Agreement

The entire region is highly vulnerable to climate change impacts. The London School of Economics estimates that across the Pacific Islands, home to 10 million people, up to 1.7 million could be displaced due to climate change by 2050. Yet Fiji, like all Pacific Island states, faces challenges in fully implementing government policies due to limited technical, human resource and financial capacities.

Support for adaptation and resilience-building, especially for the most vulnerable nations, is a priority. As a result, and next to other issues to be discussed at COP23, Prime Minister Bainimarama plans to prioritise finance for climate adaptation through the private sector.

Fiji's Specific Situation

Home to over 870,000 people in the central South Pacific Ocean, Fiji's 300 volcanic islands include low-lying atolls that are highly susceptible to cyclones and floods. Thus Fiji is no stranger to the devastation wrought by climate change.

Sea flooding is usually associated with the passage of tropical cyclones close to the coast. However, heavy swells, generated by deep depressions and/or intense high pressure systems some distance away from Fiji, have also caused flooding to low-lying coastal areas.

In 2012, Vunidogoloa became the first village to begin relocating to higher ground due to sea-level rise.

Looking to the future, the impacts of climate change on Fiji will only increase.

According to a World Bank report, climate threats to Fiji's society and economy include:

- higher rates of disease as average temperatures rise;
- increasingly destructive storms as oceans get warmer and weather patterns become more severe;
- and disruptions to agriculture as the intrusion of saltwater damages existing farmland.
- On Fiji's main island of Viti Levu, these factors are expected to contribute to economic damages of up to $52 million per year, or roughly four percent of Fiji's gross domestic product

Support by the International Community

Addressing vulnerability is thus a key concern for the country and Fiji's national policies hold valuable lessons for all governments bracing for climate-induced population movements.

The government is implementing projects to address vulnerability by increasing resilience. Projects include initiatives funded through the Global Environment

Facility (GEF), the Green Climate Fund (GCF) and with support from numerous United Nations agencies.

Together with other highly vulnerable countries, Fiji is also a member of the Climate Vulnerable Forum

Inoke Cakau, Defence Minister, had just completed reading the latest report from the United Nations Climate Change Secretariat. It disturbed him greatly. Fiji was in real jeopardy from rising sea levels and his Prime Minister discounted climate change as a greenie hoax. Something had to be done.

January 2020

Prime Minister Daurewa was in his office being briefed by his Minister for Defence on the progress of negotiations to purchase twenty-one patrol boats from an Australian consortium. Fiji would be the major recipient of the boats, but the patrol boats would be purchased by several Pacific nations.

- Papua New Guinea
- Federated States of Micronesia
- Tonga
- Solomon Islands
- Marshall Islands
- Samoa
- Vanuatu
- Timor

These nations would all be involved in the program. Fiji, being the most prosperous nation, would purchase five of the state-of-the-art vessels.

'Inoke, are the patrol boats still on schedule?' asked the Prime Minister.

'Mr Prime Minister, I am saddened to inform you that the schedule has slipped six months.'

'Six months! Last meeting we had everything was going to plan. What's happened?'

'Sir, we have been informed that the radar system, which is state-of-the-art, is taking longer to perfect than originally planned.'

'I don't care how fucking state-of-the-art it is! I want my boats and I want them by the due date.'

'I'll inform the project director of your displeasure.'

'Yes, you do that.'

'Is there any other business we need to discuss?'

'No, everything is running smoothly in the military.'

The Prime Minister's PA knocked frantically on the PM's door.

'What is it, Grace? I'm still with Inoke.'

'Sir, I need to talk to you immediately, it's urgent.'

'Very well, come in.'

'Mr Prime Minister, there are two tanks outside the Government House gates. I believe there are also tanks outside the TV station and at various other strategic locations.'

'Fuck, it's a coup! Who in the military is organising it?'

'I am, sir. You are under arrest.'

'You, my loyal Defence Minister? Why?'

'I will brief you all in good time but in the meantime, please accompany these two special forces soldiers back to the barracks. Forgive me, but I have a lot of things to organise.'

Prime Minister Daurewa came to power in a coup and now the adage "he who lives by the sword dies by the sword" had come back to haunt him.

Inoke Cakau was now Prime Minister and his principle policy was global warming. Fiji, along with the other Pacific nations, was unhappy with the major world leaders' commitment to reducing greenhouse emissions. The Pacific nations would be the first to be affected by rising sea levels. They needed to persuade America, China, India, Germany and Russia that it was in their best interests to dramatically reduce their emissions.

The problem was, how could a small island nation persuade the superpowers to reduce their greenhouse gas emissions?

TREASURE HUNT

CHAPTER 4

August 5 2020

Aurarius arrived at the port of Lautoka. Apart from the white squall, the voyage had been an uneventful one. They intended to replenish their provisions including several crates of Fiji Water, regarded as the purest spring water in the world. On board was Noa Jiko a Fijian Government representative. As part of the salvage approval the government required a representative on-board.

After two days in port, *Aurarius* headed out to open seas in pursuit of the *SS Vanderbilt's* gold.

The estimated location of the gold ship was near Tuvuca, a remote island with only one village surrounded by the Pacific Ocean.

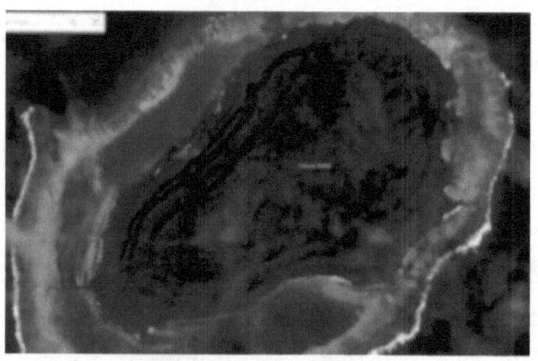

Tuvuca Island – Fiji

The search area was expansive, which would prove a real challenge for the salvage operation, but they had time on their side and the budget, thanks to Richard Manson, was extensive

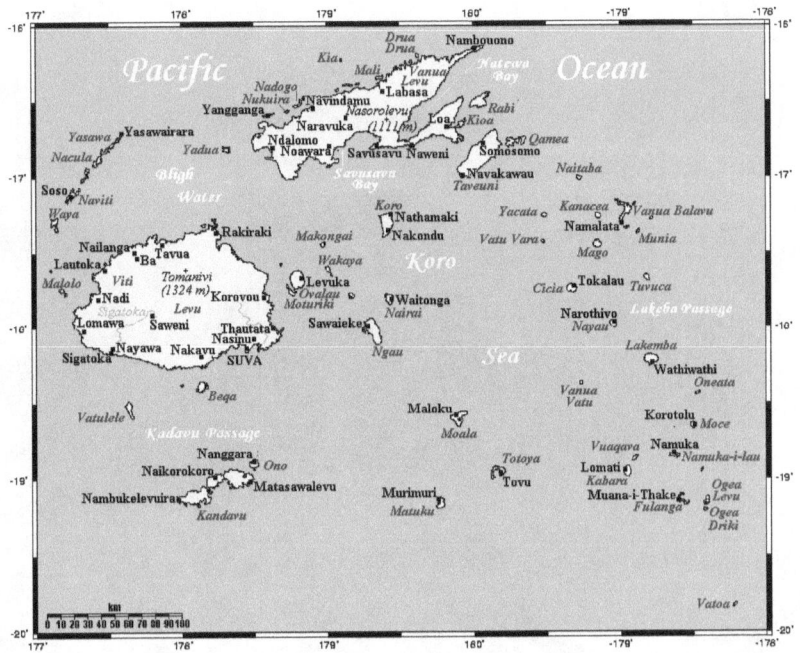

August 8 2020

Aurarius sailed out of Lautoka Harbour heading for Tuvuca Island. It would take her fifteen hours to reach the remote location.

August 9

Captain Fairweather and his first mate Adrian Hayes were checking the sonar. Noa Jiko was also in attendance.

'Everything looks in order, Captain. Shall we begin our first sweep?'

'Yes, go ahead, Adrian, I propose we travel east for ten nautical miles and then return on a parallel course.'

'Yes sir, at what speed?'

'Normal sonar speed, five knots.'

'Yes sir.'

Aurarius completed six sweeps on the first day but the sonar found nothing of significance.

The crew congregated in the ship's mess. That night, Allan White, the ship's chef, served up spaghetti Bolognese with crispy bread and salad. There was either red wine or beer to accompany the meal.

The dinner conversation centred on the first day of searching.

'Well, we didn't expect to find her on the first day I suppose,' said Captain Fairweather.

'It took seventy years of people searching before Ballard found the *Titanic*,' said Frank Caruso, the head diver.

'Well, I don't think we have that much time. It's costing Richard Manson $20,000 a day,' said First Mate George Dixon.

The next morning was perfect for the search, with calm waters and blue skies above. However, after a day of scanning the ocean floor, nothing was found.

The same pattern followed for the next two weeks. The crew had become frustrated with the lack of success.

August 24 2020

Captain Fairweather was on the bridge when the sonar operator called him on the ship's intercom.

'Captain, I think you should come down here. I think we've found something.'

'OK, I'm on my way.'

The captain entered the sonar room and looked at the screen.

'It's certainly not the *Vanderbilt* by the shape of it. Looks like a plane.'

'I think you're right, sir.'

'I'm going to launch the *IMP*. Let's see if we can get some pictures.'

Captain Fairweather gave the order to lower the *IMP*. The submersible could dive to 15,000 feet. The sonar estimated the object was at 14,000 feet, so the *IMP* was almost at its limit.

Once the submersible reached the ocean floor, a clear image confirmed the large object was a U.S. fighter plane. At last Mathew had been found.

Close by lay two objects encrusted in barnacles, but the *IMP* didn't really give a clear picture.

'OK, well there's no way we can salvage the plane but those two objects could be lifted aboard.'

The submersible operator, Garry Irvine, manoeuvred the sub to the point where the hydraulic claw could grasp the first of the objects.

'Bring her up, Garry.'

When the *IMP* finally reached the surface, it was attached to the ship's crane and lifted on board. The object was detached and the *IMP* was lowered once again to retrieve the second object.

Noa, the Fijian Government representative, was watching closely. The ship was in Fijian waters and therefore these objects were the property of the Fijian Government.

Captain Fairweather called on the German scientist Router Iffinger who was conducting scientific experiments on the voyage at the invitation of Richard Manson. His experiments would help determine ocean temperature and the rise of sea levels in the Pacific. Fairweather hoped that since Iffinger was a marine scientist, he could identify the two objects lying on the deck.

'I'm not a weapons expert, as you know, Captain, but I believe they are bombs.'

'That would make sense as, after all, the plane below is believed to be a U.S. fighter.'

Noa telephoned his superior in Fiji, informing him of the find. He didn't think his government would be interested in two bombs but he thought he should check with his superior.

Ratu Robert Bari listened to Noa's account. He decided to call the Prime Minister Inoke Cakau, who had only been in power for six weeks.

The PM was Defence Minister prior to the coup, and had been a senior officer in the armed forces for many years prior to entering politics.

When he was told of the suspected bombs and where they came from, his military antennae was immediately activated. He knew the types of bombs American fighters carried. Some were nuclear.

He instructed his defence minister to call Noa on the *Aurarius* and claim the bombs in Fiji's name. He also instructed him that the ship must return to Lautoka port and hand over the salvaged bombs.

'Captain, I have been instructed by my Prime Minister to return the bombs back to Lautoka immediately.'

'Your bombs! They are salvage and under our agreement Manson Salvage and the Fijian Government share fifty-fifty. Having said that, why the interest in a couple of barnacle-infested bombs?'

'The agreement covers discovering the *Vanderbilt* only; now I insist we return, or the Prime Minister will dispatch a patrol boat to escort the *Aurarius* back to port. Once the bombs have been unloaded you will be free to continue your search for the *Vanderbilt*.'

Captain Fairweather reluctantly agreed, as the return voyage would effectively take them away from the search for two days.

Once the salvage ship docked they were instructed to wait for nightfall. A team with a mobile crane carefully lowered the two bombs onto a truck where they were secured and driven away.

The *Aurarius* left port immediately, heading back to the search area where the search continued the next afternoon.

THE PLOT

CHAPTER 5

September 2020

The army truck with the salvaged bombs drove from Lautoka to Suva in four hours. Their destination was Queen Elizabeth Barracks. Once inside the barrack grounds, the truck drove to the far side where several soldiers were there to meet them and help unload the lethal cargo.

The building where the bombs were stored was a disused munitions warehouse, and therefore deserted.

The Prime Minister, his Defence Minister and a munitions expert arrived at the warehouse at nine the next morning.

After close examination, it was established that both bombs carried nuclear warheads. With further research, the munitions expert identified them as four-megaton bombs. This was the type of nuclear bomb carried by the Skyhawk. The plane discovered in the ocean was therefore a Skyhawk.

Prime Minister Inoke Cakau called a private meeting with his Defence Minister and the Minister for the Environment in his home office.

Prior to the two ministers arriving, he had his office swept for bugs. He was taking no chances.

The two men arrived in separate Range Rovers and were ushered into the office. A soldier used a wand over the men to ensure they were not wired.

'Mr Prime Minister, why the cloak and dagger? I thought we were your trusted ministers and friends.'

'Indeed you are, but the purpose of this meeting is so critical I had to take extra precautions. Please forgive me. The fact that only you two were summoned to this meeting is a testament to the trust I have in you both. Please sit down.'

The two men sat on the three-seater leather lounge while the Prime Minister sat in his favourite wingback.

'Gentlemen, what is Fiji's greatest threat?'

'Well, it's certainly not the other Pacific Island groups,' said George Finau, the Defence Minister.

'It could be China investing in our natural resources,' said George.

'You're not saying anything, Emori. What do you think our greatest threat is?'

'I might be biased, sir, but I would suggest global warming is our greatest threat.'

'Ah ha, you've got it, Emori. If the Earth's temperature continues to rise at its current rate, Fiji won't exist in thirty years' time.

'We must stop this global warming madness.'

'But Fiji produces virtually no CO_2 emissions, so how can we have any impact?' asked George.

'That is why I called you here. The plan I am about to outline must remain confidential; your lives depend on it.

"We all agree Fiji is in great danger from rising sea levels as a result of global warming. As you are aware, we are not in a position of strength to influence the big polluters.

"Serendipity has played a hand in our cause. We are now in possession of two four-megaton atomic bombs recovered from the wreck of an American jet fighter.

31

"There is sufficient Plutonium 239 in these two bombs to manufacture six one-megaton bombs.

"The plan is to place a bomb in New York, New Delhi, Beijing, Berlin and Moscow. We have no plans to explode any of them. We will be using them to leverage our case.'

'I count five. What about the sixth?' asked George Finau.

'That will be the only bomb which will be detonated. We will place it on a barge and tow it to a remote part of the Pacific where no harm can be done. We will announce our intention to the world's press prior to detonation. This demonstration should put the wind up the world leaders and encourage them to act quickly.'

'So what demands will we make?' asked Emori.

'As you are both aware, the Paris agreement was way short of our hopes for a sustainable agreement.

'We will demand the agreement be strengthened.'

The key elements of the Paris agreement were:

- To keep global temperatures "well below" 2.0C (3.6F) above pre-industrial times and "endeavour to limit" them even more, to 1.5C

We demand 1.0C

- To limit the amount of greenhouse gases emitted by human activity to the same levels that trees, soil and oceans can absorb naturally, beginning at some point between 2050 and 2100

We demand by 2020

- To review each country's contribution to cutting emissions every five years so they scale up to the challenge

We demand annual reviews

- For rich countries to help poorer nations by providing "climate finance" to adapt to climate change and switch to renewable energy.

We demand to see evidence on an ongoing basis.

'They are noble objectives, Mr Prime Minister, but threatening the world with a nuclear holocaust would place Fiji in a very precarious position. As you know our defence force is minuscule compared to those we threaten,' said George.

'I agree, George; we need to ensure Fiji is not connected with this operation. We must distance ourselves from anything to do with this plan. We are simply observers.'

'How do we accomplish that?'

'Firstly, we establish a clandestine group; environmental terrorists if you will. I propose we call it the "Environmental Defence Organisation".

'The EDO would be run at arm's length but controlled by us. We will have military officers on the inside.'

'May I bring up another point, sir? How are we going to build these bombs? No one in Fiji would have the expertise.'

'You are right, George; I propose you travel to North Korea on a goodwill mission. Since Kim Jong-un disbanded the country's nuclear program they have nuclear scientists twiddling their thumbs. If we offer them a significant fee I'm sure they would come here and build the bombs.'

'The crew of the *Aurarius* know we recovered the two bombs. They must suspect they were nuclear, so how do we maintain their silence?' asked Emori.

'That issue is being taken care of as we speak. We won't have to worry about them.'

'What do you mean?'

'We are negotiating with them to keep their silence.'

'Do you think they will?'

'Yes, I'm sure they will see reason.'

'What about Richard Manson? He is sure to know about the salvaged bombs.'

'He too is being spoken to.'

'I hope this is worth it.'

'Fiji's very existence is relying on our success. It's worth it.'

SILENCE IS GOLDEN

CHAPTER 6

The Fijian patrol boat departed Togalevu Naval Base at 1am so as not to bring attention to her leaving of the harbour. On board were six naval crew and six Fijian SAS soldiers. The voyage would take eight hours and the destination was top secret.

The seas were choppy but the Israeli-manufactured vessel took it all in her stride.

After eight hours they began looking for their target, and after two hours searching, a crewman spotted the *Aurarius*.

Patrol Boat 203 pulled up alongside; the captain notified Captain Fairweather it was their intention to board.

'What do you think they want sir?' asked the first mate.

'I would think it's just a routine check for drug smuggling or similar. We just need to be polite and let them go about their business.'

The patrol boat's commanding officer and six SAS Rangers boarded the boat's Odyssey to enable them to board the Aurarius. Once aboard, the officer climbed up to the bridge. One SAS Ranger accompanied him.

The remainder of the boarding party asked all crew to gather at the stern of the ship.

The captain and the first mate were occupying the bridge.

'Good morning, Captain Fairweather. My name is George Bari. I am the commander of patrol boat 203.'

'Good morning. How can I help you?'

'Actually, Captain, I don't need your help.'

The patrol boat's officer pulled out his SIG Sauer and shot Fairweather in the forehead at the same time the SAS Ranger shot the first mate.

The agreement was when the SAS Rangers heard the shots they would open fire with their Uzi submachine guns. Soon twelve bodies lay crumpled and bleeding on the deck.

Stage one was complete. Stage two was to place explosives below deck. When detonated, the *Aurarius* would sink to the ocean floor.

The team worked quickly. They knew what they were doing and once it was completed, they reboarded the Odyssey and return to the patrol boat.

The patrol boat moved 500 metres from the *Aurarius* and detonated the charges. The noise was deafening. Fire erupted all over the ship and within twenty minutes she was gone below the water without a trace.

Richard Manson was a creature of habit. After lunch each workday, he would don his Nike walking shoes and walk up Madison Avenue to Park Avenue where he turned right. Then he turned down W42 Street and then 5th Avenue until he reached Madison Avenue once again. It was a three-mile walk, which kept him fit and gave him time alone to think.

Richard was walking along W42 Street when a Ford SUV mounted the footpath and struck Richard at speed. The police later estimated the truck was doing seventy miles an hour. Richard was killed instantly, and the SUV disappeared without a trace.

It was reported back to Prime Minister Cakau that the second stage of the project was completed without incident.

He was now confident that his top-secret project would remain under cover.

The soldiers who unloaded the bombs were unaware of the contents of the crates so they were not a threat and therefore remained safe.

The next critical step was to arrange for George Finau, the Defence Minister, to travel to North Korea and recruit the nuclear scientists needed to construct the bombs.

A reservation was made departing Suva for Sydney, Australia. He then flew to Canberra for a meeting with his Australian counterpart Dennis Short. The stopover was meant to make his trip look like one of diplomacy.

Finau then flew with Qantas to Beijing where he had two meetings in the Chinese capital; one with the Defence Minister and another with the Minister for the Environment. His final leg was to Pyongyang, North Korea, where he would meet several senior defence personnel.

His main objective was to meet with the retired head of nuclear science, Mr Jan Song Take, on the pretence that Fiji was considering nuclear energy as its main source of electric power generation. His request was granted. Jan Song Take was now a senior professor at North Korea's top university, Pyongyang University of Science and Technology. A meeting was set up on the university grounds.

George was aware that anything discussed in the meeting would be taped, therefore; he recorded the Prime Minister's proposal on a thumb drive. His intention was to clandestinely pass the thumb drive to the professor during their meeting.

George was nervous. He knew if he were caught he would go to gaol or even worse be shot as a spy. The risk was worth it if he could help save Fiji from annihilation.

The meeting was scheduled for Tuesday at 10am. A government car picked up the Defence Minister from the Pyongyang Hotel where he was staying.

It was only a fifteen-minute drive to the university's campus. George was escorted to a meeting room and instructed to wait.

'The professor will join you shortly. Please take a seat,' said one of the guards.

The two men left the room.

George complied. It was a sparsely furnished room with a single window looking out to the common green.

After a ten-minute wait, Professor Jan Song-Taek entered the room, greeting George warmly. George was pleasantly surprised that the only other person present was a translator.

Once the pleasantries were out of the way George explained the purpose of his visit.

'Professor, you are regarded as one of the top nuclear scientists in the world. Fiji is seriously considering nuclear power as its main source of electricity generation. We would like to offer you and a team of nuclear scientists of your choosing the opportunity of coming to Fiji to design suitable power plants. We would pay you handsomely as well as compensating the North Korean Government.'

'You flatter me, Mr Finau. I must admit I do miss the hands-on as it were. You understand my government would need to approve the assignment and I would need to know more details, but if approved, I would be happy to assist you.'

'That's excellent, Professor. I look forward to hearing from you once your government has decided.'

The two men stood up and shook hands. George had the thumb drive in his palm and Professor Taek took it and placed it in his right pocket.

George returned to his hotel. His flight to Beijing was the following morning.

When the professor arrived at his apartment at the end of the day, he inserted the thumb drive into his computer.

In essence, the documents outlined Fiji's plan to manufacture six atomic weapons to be used as bargaining chips with the world's superpowers to act more quickly on reducing greenhouse gases.

Professor Taek's initial reaction was shock, but after assessing the reasons for the weapons, he decided it was a noble cause.

Professor Taek communicated with the Fijian Government, using encrypted email. He was a trusted citizen, but in North Korea, one never knows who's listening.

Dear Mr Finau,

I have considered your offer to build a nuclear power plant for your government.

I am pleased to inform you that I accept subject to the approval of my government.

You would be required to build a secure laboratory for my team of six scientists to conduct the design work and the handling of nuclear material to be used in the reactor.

The North Korean Government have intimated they would require a fee if US$20,000,000 to release me and my team. Included in the fee would be existing plans, which should expedite the construction.

Please get back to me when it is convenient.

Yours sincerely,

Jan Song-Taek

Department Head

George printed the email and filed it in a secret folder on his computer. He telephoned the prime minister, requesting a meeting, which was duly granted.

He didn't have to wait long in the PM's reception area. Inoke was keen to hear George's news.

'Hello George, take a seat. Can I get Lucy to bring us coffee?'

'No, not for me, Mr Prime Minister. I have received an email from Jan Song-Taek.'

'Well, what does he say?'

George passed the email over to his prime minister, who read it carefully.

'$20,000,000 is a significant amount of money in anyone's language. Do we know how much we need to pay the North Korean scientific team?'

'Not yet but I would imagine $2,000,000 a bomb is likely.'

'This is becoming an expensive exercise and we also need to build the secure lab.'

'Sir, with due respect, if we started from scratch it would probably cost one billion a bomb.'

'You're right of course. We can't lose sight of what we aim to achieve. So what's the next step?'

'We are waiting on the North Korean Government to approve the project. They're not known for their quick decisions. I also need to negotiate the design and build price with Mr Song-Taek.'

'OK, George; please keep me informed.'

George Finau left the PM's office and returned to his own on the other side of the Parliamentary Building.

George finally received a letter from Mr Park Khang, Head of Department, Institute of Atomic Physics.

Dear Minister Finau,

The Democratic People's Republic of North Korea has agreed to your request to provide six nuclear scientists and engineering drawings to enable Fiji to construct a nuclear power plant in your country.

Please be beware the investment North Korea has made in nuclear technology has been significant. It is with this in mind that we request a payment of $20,000,000. The contract fee for the scientists can be negotiated separately.

If you accept our terms we would be able to begin the project in the next month.

Yours sincerely,

Yong Park Hang

Head of Department Institute of Atomic Physics

George requested another meeting with his prime minister to discuss the next step.

'As you are now aware, sir, the North Koreans have approved our request for the team of nuclear scientists to travel and stay here indefinitely.

'I have been researching the best site to build the bombs and have decided that Bilo, on the outskirts of Suva, would be the ideal location. As you are aware it is deep under the mountain and has been used recently as an ammunition magazine. To convert some of the caverns to a nuclear lab wouldn't take an enormous effort.'

'Can you organise a site visit for myself and Emori tomorrow? It's important we all agree on a suitable location.'

'Yes of cause, sir, I'll arrange it.'

The next morning the three ministers drove out to Bilo a thirty-minute road trip. They entered the tunnel, stopping deep into the mountain. Bilo had been constructed during World War 2 as a safe haven against the invading Japanese.

All three were impressed with the state the cavern was in. It wouldn't take too much renovation to create a clean state-of-the-art nuclear lab.

Prime Minister Cakau approved the expenditure immediately, instructing George and Emori to organise the work to begin ASAP.

The story they told the press was that the cavern was going to be used to create vaccines; hence the need for a sealed clean laboratory.

The renovations took three months and all was now ready for the work to begin.

Bilo Nuclear laboratory

HOW TO BUILD AN ATOMIC BOMB

CHAPTER 7

Pyongyang North Korea

Professor Jan Song Taek was sitting in his office running through the plan in his mind. He dare not take notes as these could be used as evidence against him.

He had been successful in recruiting five more nuclear scientists willing to travel to Fiji for the purpose of building six nuclear bombs.

They were:

Daeshim Kim

Jintao Gim

Seung Lee

Yong – Sun Rhee

Young – Ja Park

Young – Jae Chung

All these scientists had been actively involved in the North Korean nuclear weapons program.

The Fijian Government had received permission from the North Koreans to second the scientists to Fiji for the purpose of building a nuclear reactor. The fee for service had been transferred to the bank account specified by the North Koreans, in the name of Kim Jong-un.

Professor Jan Song Taek had negotiated with Fiji's Defence Minister, agreeing his team would be paid $2,500.000 per bomb. They also required suitable living quarters for the duration of their stay.

The six scientists caught a flight to Beijing. They then boarded a Fiji Air flight to Nadi. George Finau arranged for them to be driven to Suva in a minibus by one of his trusted lieutenants.

They booked into the Quest Apartments, a four-star hotel in central Suva.

The next morning the group was taken by minibus to the Bilo laboratory and given the grand tour. They were all impressed with the facility.

George and Emori showed the team into the room where the two atomic bombs were located individually on stainless steel benches.

'It is impossible for us to determine how degraded these weapons are without dismantling them. I suggest we commence straight away,' said Jan Song Taek.

'Yes, I think that's a good idea, Professor. We'll leave you to it.'

The two ministers were quite happy to leave the room.

The scientists gently unscrewed the nose cone, detaching it from the main body of the bomb. The thermonuclear mechanism was located in the cone.

Once they completed that task, they needed to expose the bomb itself, hoping all the components were salvageable.

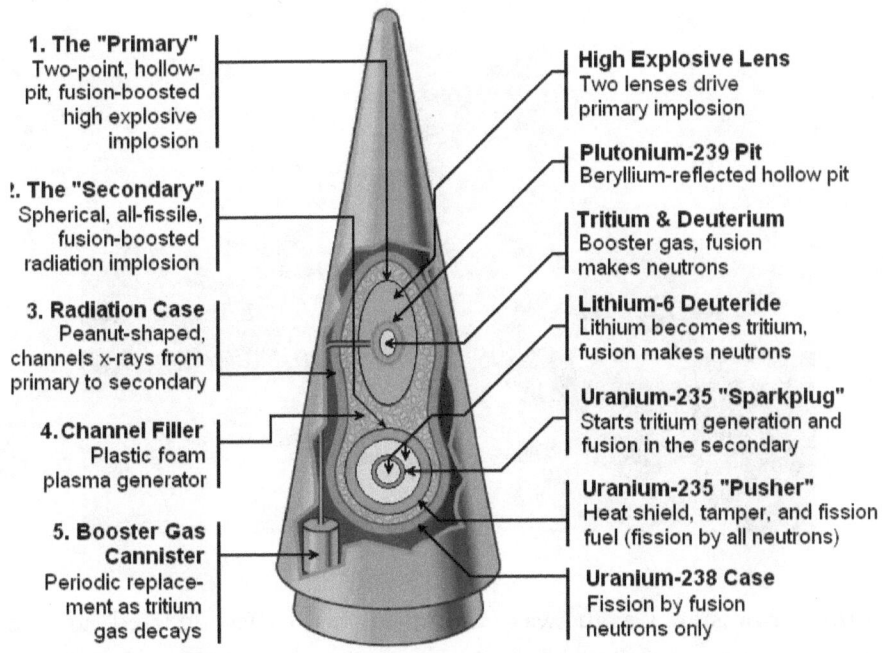

1. The "Primary"
Two-point, hollow-pit, fusion-boosted high explosive implosion

!. The "Secondary"
Spherical, all-fissile, fusion-boosted radiation implosion

3. Radiation Case
Peanut-shaped, channels x-rays from primary to secondary

4. Channel Filler
Plastic foam plasma generator

5. Booster Gas Cannister
Periodic replacement as tritium gas decays

High Explosive Lens
Two lenses drive primary implosion

Plutonium-239 Pit
Beryllium-reflected hollow pit

Tritium & Deuterium
Booster gas, fusion makes neutrons

Lithium-6 Deuteride
Lithium becomes tritium, fusion makes neutrons

Uranium-235 "Sparkplug"
Starts tritium generation and fusion in the secondary

Uranium-235 "Pusher"
Heat shield, tamper, and fission fuel (fission by all neutrons)

Uranium-238 Case
Fission by fusion neutrons only

The bomb seemed to be in perfect order. The plutonium from the first bomb was carefully extracted from its housing and placed in a lead-lined container.

The team repeated the exercise with the second bomb.

The North Koreans were satisfied. There were eighty pounds of Plutonium in all, which meant they could use ten pounds in each bomb with a twenty-pound surplus if needed.

The challenge was to construct six thermonuclear weapons small enough to fit into a suitcase.

Apart from having right material i.e. Plutonium, Uranium, Lithium, Tritium and Deuteride, the casing was the most critical element in constructing a small atomic bomb.

The build team designed a bomb, which was 273 mm in diameter and 400 mm long. The estimated weight was twenty-three kilograms, the maximum suitcase weight for an economy air ticket.

Parliament House Suva

Prime Minister Cakau was sitting in his office located in the parliamentary precinct. Waiting in his anteroom was the North Korean ambassador. Inoke suspected the reason for the meeting and wasn't particularly looking forward to it.

I might as well get it over with, he thought.

He buzzed his PA, asking her to show the ambassador in.

'Good morning, Mr Ambassador. Please take a seat.'

'Thank you, Mr Prime Minister.'

Neither man would think of using first names as it wasn't that type of relationship on a personal or diplomatic basis.

'Can I get you a tea or coffee?'

'Yes, coffee, please; one sugar and black.'

'Now may I ask the purpose of your visit?'

'As you are aware, six of our best nuclear scientists have been seconded to design and build a nuclear power station for the Fijian Government.'

'Yes, that's right and they are doing a wonderful job.'

'My government is concerned that very little work has taken place. It is our understanding no site has been selected let alone earthworks commenced.'

'Jan Song Taek and his team have been designing the reactor; that in itself as you would well know is a formable task. I'm sure you are aware Fiji is an active volcanic group of islands so we have to be absolutely sure we select the right site.'

'So our scientists are being gainfully employed?'

'They certainly are. We have paid your government a sizable fee so it is in our best interests that the scientific team is being fully utilised.'

'Thank you, Mr Prime Minister, I'll report back to my government.'

'Good morning, Mr Ambassador.'

Inoke was pleased as to how the meeting went, knowing it could have been a lot worse.

His next meeting was with his co-conspirators George and Emori to receive a progress report on the development of the bombs.

The Prime Minister had a fifteen-minute gap to read emails and check his Twitter account.

'Mr Prime Minister, the Defence Minister and the Minister for the Environment are here to see you,' said Lucy over the intercom.

45

'Send them in please, Lucy.'

When the men entered, he said, 'Hello George, hello Emori; take a seat. Can I get Lucy to bring you something?'

'Just a water please Mr Prime Minister,' said George.

'I'll have one too please, Lucy.'

'Now what's this Mr Prime Minister business? My name is Inoke as you well know.

The two men received their bottles of Fiji Water and Lucy left the room. Inoke turned off the intercom just to be sure anything said in his office remained in his office.

'Right, gentlemen; where are we at?'

'Jan Song and his team have extracted all the material which is now safely stored in suitable containers.

The housing mechanisms have now been completed and all that is required now is to build the devices. When I say all that is required; this stage is the most difficult,' said Emori.

'How long to build all six?'

'Jan Song estimates another month.'

'That's not too bad. In principle we could begin our campaign in a couple of months,' said Inoke. 'As you are both aware I've just completed a meeting with the North Korean Ambassador. He has shown concern about the lack of progress building the reactor. I think we need to start building it. Even if it is a bogus nuclear plant, the North Koreans will be satisfied as will be our allies in the region.'

'I'll arrange for the excavation work immediately.'

'That's excellent, thank you, George.

'We need to introduce EDO to the world as soon as possible using social media. It's imperative that the governments of the planet are aware that the Environmental Defence Organisation is an environmental terrorist group that will stop at nothing to minimise global warming,' said George.

'Yes, I agree. Can I leave that with you two? We can't trust anybody else to handle this.'

SOCIAL MEDIA

CHAPTER 8

George and Emori spent the following week learning all there was to know about how to effectively use Facebook. At the end of the week they were ready to post their first message.

The Facebook post attracted 10,000 likes and got the attention of the secret service agencies of the countries identified as the major polluters.

The EDO posted again the following week.

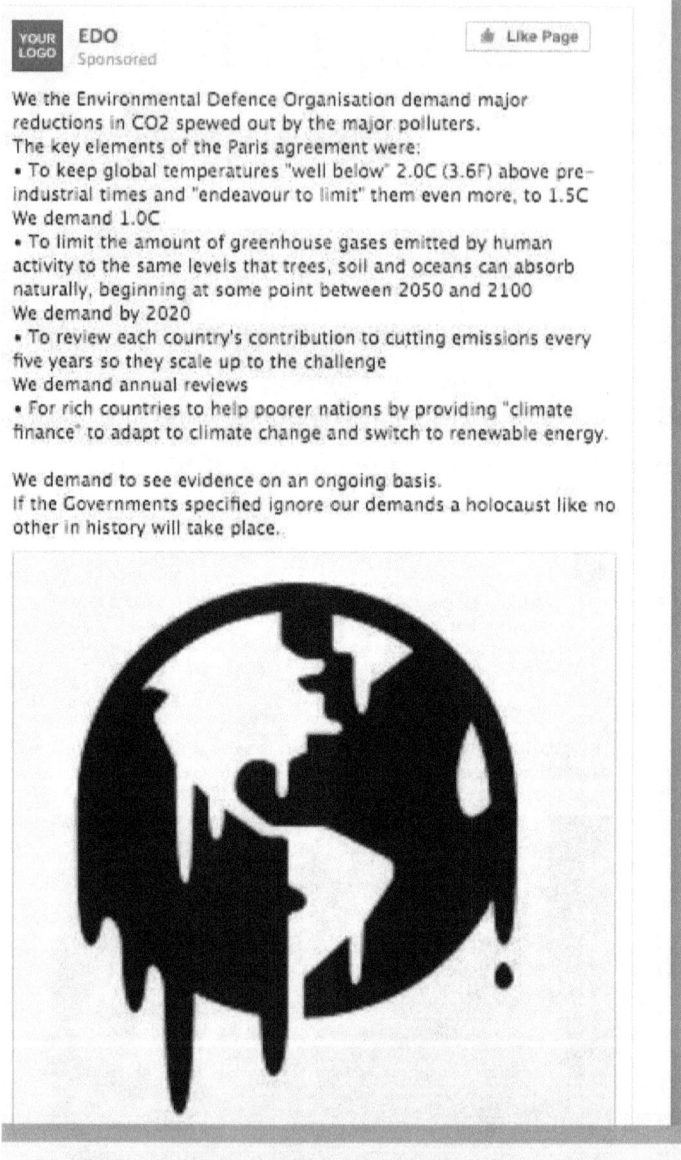

EDO
Sponsored
          👍 Like Page

We the Environmental Defence Organisation demand major reductions in CO2 spewed out by the major polluters.
The key elements of the Paris agreement were:
• To keep global temperatures "well below" 2.0C (3.6F) above pre-industrial times and "endeavour to limit" them even more, to 1.5C
We demand 1.0C
• To limit the amount of greenhouse gases emitted by human activity to the same levels that trees, soil and oceans can absorb naturally, beginning at some point between 2050 and 2100
We demand by 2020
• To review each country's contribution to cutting emissions every five years so they scale up to the challenge
We demand annual reviews
• For rich countries to help poorer nations by providing "climate finance" to adapt to climate change and switch to renewable energy.

We demand to see evidence on an ongoing basis.
If the Governments specified ignore our demands a holocaust like no other in history will take place.

The second posting attracted 1,500,000 likes. It was becoming viral; the press was becoming interested as were several foreign governments.

Once television reports began to hit the airwaves the interest of the public and government officials skyrocketed. Although the threat wasn't specified, the image of an atomic blast put a chill up everybody's spine.

Langley, CIA HQ

Langley Virginia

October 2020

The Deputy Director of the CIA for Operations, Bernard Wallace, requested a meeting with the Director of the Central Intelligence Agency, Lewis Pentecost. His request was granted.

'Good afternoon, Bernie; may I arrange a coffee? I'm afraid the sun isn't over the yardarm quite yet.'

'I'm fine sir, I had one not so long ago.'

'OK, well let's cut to the chase. What is it you want to discuss with me?'

'My department has been keeping a close eye on a group calling themselves the Environmental Defence Organisation, commonly known as the EDO.'

'Who are they? A group of aggressive greenies?'

'You could say that. I would like to show you some Facebook postings.'

The director read the postings with a concerned expression.

'Are these bastards for real or is it just a hoax?'

'That's what we are endeavouring to find out, sir.'

'They talk about a holocaust and there's an image of an atomic bomb. Not even The Muslim Army was able to build a bomb. Apart from obtaining the uranium or plutonium, it would be almost impossible to find the right people to build the fucking thing,' said Pentecost.

'I agree with you sir but we can't ignore the threat, no matter how far-fetched.'

'What do you propose?'

'The first step is already underway. We are endeavouring to identify who is posting these messages. We have requested Facebook's help in this but it seems the terrorists are able to create new accounts daily from different countries around the globe.'

'Are you aware of any enriched uranium or plutonium going missing of late?'

'No sir, not that we are aware of; although, I wouldn't put it past the North Koreans or Iranians to sell a suitable quantity to anybody that's willing to pay them enough.'

'Keep me posted, Bernie; it may just be a prank but then again...'

'I will, sir; do you want a regular briefing or only if there's something to report?'

'Just when you've got something to tell me, thanks.'

Thames House London

MI5 Head Quarters

Alan Turner, the Deputy Director General of MI5, was reading a report from one of his operatives regarding the Environmental Defence Organisation. Normally groups such as this were investigated but not elevated to Director level. What made this group different was the intimation that they were in possession of an atomic bomb. It appeared that EDO hadn't claimed possession, but its threats together with an image of an atomic bomb blast had him worried.

He decided to elevate it to his Director General Michael Lloyd.

Turner and Lloyd had joined MI5 on the same day twenty years before, so they were on very close terms.

Turner called his Director-General.

'Hello, Michael, it's Alan; may I request a meeting? There's something very important I need to discuss with you.'

'Certainly, old chum. I have an hour at 4 pm would that suit you?'

'That would be excellent; see you then.'

Turner was waiting in his director's anteroom at 4 pm. He was kept waiting for twenty minutes, but finally he was ushered into the DG's office.

'I am so sorry, Alan, I received a call from the Prime Minister at the last minute.'

'So the Prime Minister has precedence over me?'

'Yes, I'm afraid he does.'

Both men chuckled.

'So, Andrew, what would you like to discuss with me?'

Turner briefed his old friend with as much detail as he could.

'That all sounds a bit ominous. Do you really think they're serious? An atomic bomb is not something you'd build in your garage.'

'Good question and to be honest I don't know. I suggest you call Lewis Pentecost at the CIA and get his view on things.'

'That's a good idea. I'll call him after you leave.

51

Once the Deputy Director General departed, Michael asked his PA to telephone Lewis Pentecost Director of the CIA.

'Hello, Lewis it's been a long time since we spoke. How are you?'

'Hi, Michael; yes too long. I'm fine. What can I do for you?'

'My team are concerned with a group calling themselves the Environmental Defence Organisation. Have you heard of them?'

'I got briefed only yesterday. I'm not sure what to make of them. If they're serious we have a real problem on our hands, we all do.'

'It's not just America they have in their sights. They have also targeted India, China, Germany and Japan.'

'I take it Britain wasn't one of the countries threatened, so why are you taking such a strong interest?'

'Britain is part of Europe so any threat to it is a threat to us.'

'Don't get me wrong, Michael; any help from MI5 is most welcome.'

'So we both agree any information we can gather on this organisation will be shared?'

'Absolutely, Lewis; I intend to contact Germany so may I suggest you contact India and Russia.'

'Agreed.'

'Goodbye Lewis, and let's hope the next time we speak it will be a social chat.'

'One can only hope, Michael, but seeing we both head up the biggest and most powerful intelligence agencies in the world I think it unlikely.'

'I think you're right. Goodbye.'

Michael Lloyd rang his German counterpart Karl Weber, Director of the Federal Intelligence Service based in Berlin.

The Germans were aware of the EDO and were trying to track down where they were located.

The Russians were also pursuing the environmental terrorist group and were keen to share information.

Environmental Defence Organisation (EDO) Is a Serios Threat to Global Warming Apathy
Sponsored

Intelligence agencies all over the world are searching for EDO. Forget it you'll never find us.

Citizens you need to pressure your Governments to act noow

If EDO does not see concrete evidence by July 1 we will detonate the first bomb

EDO IS NOT A TERRORIST ORGANISATION

Learn More

203K

120K Comments   50K Shares

Like   Comment   Share

'If they are so fucking smart you think they'd know how to spell,' said Lewis Pentecost to his Deputy.

'They may not know how to spell but they're pretty good at getting attention. Thirty million likes, one million comments and twenty million shares; that's a lot of people who now know about EDO,' said Bernard Wallace.

'You're right, Bernard; we have three days to find these bastards and so far we have no concrete leads. Neither do MI5 or any of the others. I'm starting to get nervous. God knows what they've got planned for the 1st of July.

WE SAID WE WERE SERIOUS

CHAPTER 9

Suva Fiji

01 June 2021

Inoke Cakau was sitting at his desk reading the final report from Jan Song Taek. In it, he reported that the six nuclear devices were now ready to be deployed.

The Prime Minister had already authorised $15,000,000 to Jan Song and his team.

He placed his head in his hands.

'Please God, am I doing the right thing? I'm only trying to save my country from ruin.'

He stood up and began pacing his office talking to himself.

'We've come this far. No nuclear device will be detonated in any of the five countries we are targeting; we are just using them as a big stick to get them to act.'

His PA buzzed to inform him George and Emori were in the anteroom.

'Tell them to come in, Lucy.'

He looked up as they entered. 'Hello, gentlemen; please take a seat.'

He didn't offer refreshments; no time for that.

'So gentlemen, I have been informed by the scientific team that we have six nuclear devices in our possession. The demonstration of our strength will take place on July 1.

'The nuclear device is ready to be towed to the detonation site.'

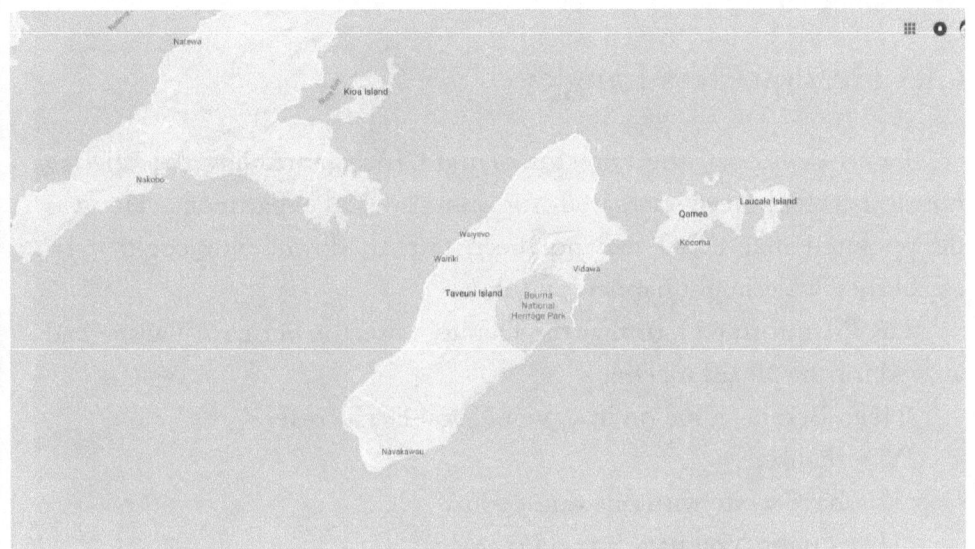

The site is a hundred nautical miles off of Taveuni and the barge will be towed by my launch.

'Excuse me, sir, is that far enough away from Taveuni? The last thing we want to do is harm our own.'

'I have been informed by the experts that twenty miles would be the maximum danger zone.

'EDO will put out a press release announcing the event with the GPS coordinates so that reconnaissance satellites could view and record the explosion for the whole world to see.'

'When will our diplomats deliver the suitcases to their destinations?' asked Emori.

'They have already begun. One of our men has stored the device in the basement of our embassy in Berlin.'

'Excellent. He had no problem with customs?'

'None. Being a diplomatic case, it was passed through without being X-rayed.'

'What about the other locations?'

'They will all be in place within the next fortnight.'

'Will they all be placed in our embassies?'

'Yes, the various authorities cannot enter an embassy uninvited.'

Washington DC

CIA Headquarters Langley

Lewis Pentecost, the Director of the CIA, was reading the briefing notes that had been prepared for him by his department. He was disappointed that EDO had not been tracked down. Nor could it be established what might happen on July1.

His PA informed him that the Deputy Director Bernard Wallace had arrived for the 10 am meeting.

'Hello Bernie, come on in… would you like a coffee?'

'Yes, thanks.'

'You have white with one don't you.'

'That's right. You have a good memory.'

'Come on, Bernie, how long have we known each other?'

'A long time, Lewis.'

'While we wait for our coffees, have you got any more intelligence on this crazy EDO rabble?'

'I'm afraid I don't. They are more sophisticated than we first thought. They're covering their tracks very well and if I didn't know better I would guess it's a foreign government.'

'I take it MI5 and the others are having difficulty as well?'

'That's right; they have no idea.'

'Do we have any inkling what they plan for July 1?'

'None whatsoever. It could be a car bomb or an attack on a famous attraction such as the Louvre. All the named governments will be stepping up their security on the day. Have you briefed the president yet?'

'No, until I know what we are up against I think it would be premature.'

July 1

2021

Chapter 10

July 1 2021

Pacific Ocean

The barge with the nuclear bomb had been tethered by anchor and the patrol boat had withdrawn thirty miles. All was ready; the only thing left to do was to press the button that would detonate the device.

Captain Levenei Apolosi was standing by to receive the final approval. His satellite phone rang. The Fijian Prime Minister gave his approval.

The captain pushed the button.

The world watched in awe.

President Cooper had an only son; his wife Barbara and he had hoped for more children but it was not to be.

The President's son was named Lucas. He was married to Anna and they had two children, ten-year-old Luke and Sophie, who was two years younger.

The family was enjoying a Fijian holiday at Matangi Private Island Resort, a five-star establishment on a small island off Tavenui Island.

They were enjoying the beach; the water was crystal clear and the temperature was 29 degrees Celsius. Lucas Cooper was lying on a sun lounge reading a Robert Ludlum novel, *The Bourne Deception*. Anna was reading *Emma,* by Jane Austin. Luke and Sophie were playing in the water.

Luke noticed a wave in the distance about. It was five feet high and it was moving fast.

'Dad, can you see that wave out there?'

Lucas put down his book, stood up and walked to the water's edge, and looked out to sea.

'My God, I think it's a tsunami! Quick, everybody, get off the beach!' he yelled.

The Cooper family and all those on the beach ran for the main resort building, but by the time they had reached the building, the tsunami had caught them. Furniture was being washed away as were several guests and hotel staff.

The Cooper family held onto the posts supporting the roof of the restaurant.

A large piece of furniture slammed into Lucas. He lost his grip and disappeared. He was found two days later.

The atomic bomb triggered an earthquake which created the tsunami and killed fifty people. This was not part of the plan. No one was meant to get hurt.

The fact that the President of the United States' son was one of the casualties brought it up another level.

Washington DC

President Donald Cooper was in the situation room in the White House. As President of the National Security Council, he viewed the nuclear explosion in the Pacific Ocean with the other members of the council.

Present were:
Vice President Graham Anderson
Secretary of State William Morris
Secretary of Defence Michelle Bennett
Secretary of Energy David Murphy
Secretary of the Treasury Ian Bryant

Also in the room, although not a member of the NSC, was the Secretary of the Environment.

'What the fuck is going on here? How could we have missed this?'

'Sir, we have been aware of this terrorist group for some time, but unfortunately, we have not been able to locate them,' said Michelle Bennett.

'Why isn't Pentecost here? He's the one that's been telling me for years that no terrorist group could manufacture an atomic bomb.'

'I'll call him, sir,' said Vice President Anderson.

'What are they demanding?'

'I have copies of the Facebook posts they have been posting if you wish to peruse them,' said the Secretary of Defence.

Lewis Pentecost asked permission to enter the situation room and the President pushed the button, allowing entry.

There were no pleasantries.

'Lewis, this is your fuck-up. What have you got to say for yourself?'

'Sir, I can only apologise; we have been trying to locate this terrorist group for the past three months. I will say in my defence the intelligence agencies of Britain, Germany, Russia, India and China have been desperately trying to find this group also but, none of them have been successful,' said Pentecost.

'Do we know where these bastards got hold of the plutonium?'

'We have checked every nuclear reactor under our control as have the other four countries being threatened. No plutonium is missing. '

'Well, even if they could steal enough plutonium they need the scientific expertise to build the fucking thing. There's got to be a trail surely,' said the president.

The president's telephone rang.

'For God's sake, this better be important. I left instructions I was not to be disturbed.' He picked up the telephone. It was his wife.

'Donald, I need to talk to you as soon as possible. It's important, darling.'

'I'll call a break now. I'll see you in the sitting room. What's wrong, Emma?'

'I'll tell you when I see you.'

The president put the telephone down. He looked concerned.

'OK, everybody; we'll take a thirty-minute break. The president left the room immediately.

He entered the elaborate room to find his wife looking out the bay window to the rose gardens. She turned and walked towards him, tears streaming down her face.

The White House Sitting Room

'What's wrong, darling?'

'The Fijian tsunami hit the resort where Lucas and the family were staying.'

'Oh my God, are they OK?'

'Anna and the kids are fine a few scratches and bruises.'

'What about Lucas?'

'He got swept away they found his body this morning.'

The president didn't say a word. He was totally dumbfounded.

'Donald, say something.'

'What can I say? I've lost my son. Apart from you he was the person I most loved in the world and now he's gone.'

The couple hugged each other both cried and consoled and cried some more.

'I can promise you this, Emma. I will catch whoever did this.'

'It was a natural disaster, darling.'

'No it wasn't. It was a terrorist group that detonated a nuclear bomb; that's what did this, and I declare if it's the last thing I do I will bring them to justice.'

Donald Cooper phoned down to the Situation Room cancelling the meeting until further notice.

MI5

CHAPTER 11

Thames House London

Michael Lloyd, Director General of MI5, and his executive team had just witnessed a nuclear explosion and they were gobsmacked. Not since Hiroshima and Nagasaki had a thermal nuclear device exploded in anger.

'What do we do now?' asked Deputy General Alan Turner.

'We catch these bastards before they start exploding nuclear bombs in our major cities,' said Lloyd.

'With respect, sir, we have been looking for this terrorist group for the past three months without success,' said Turner.

'Well, this is now our number one priority. We must find these reprobates.'

'The whole world has seen the vision. Even the Queen has expressed her concern.'

'Do we have any idea where they obtained the plutonium?' asked Michael Lloyd.

'There are a number of options, sir; they could have stolen a disused nuclear bomb or they could have smuggled it out of a nuclear power plant,' said Turner.

'We need to call the executive group together as soon as possible. Alan, can you organise it?'

'Of course, sir. Do you want the whole team?'

'No, just the relevant department heads initially.'

The group comprised:

Deputy Director - General

International Counter-Terrorism

Deputy Director Capability

Deputy Director Strategy

'We may need to bring in the total group a little later on.'

'Yes, sir. When would you like to organise it?'

'Tonight.'

'Right, I'd better get onto it.'

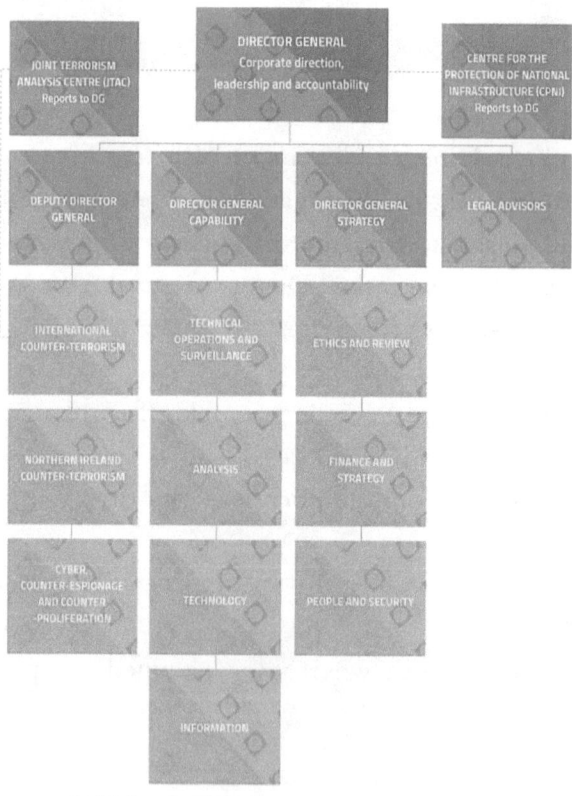

MI5 Senior Management Structure

The nuclear explosion had caused a similar response around the world.

Moscow

The President of Russia, Alexander Ivanov, was presiding over his war cabinet.

Russian War Room

In the room were:

Boris Smirnov Directorate KR: External Counter-Intelligence: infiltration of foreign intelligence and security services and exercising surveillance over Russian citizens abroad.

Egor Kuznetsov Directorate OT: Operational and Technical Support

Feodore Popov Directorate R: Operational Planning and Analysis: Evaluates SVR operations abroad.

Gavrie Vasiliev Directorate I: Computer Service (Information and Dissemination): Analyzes and distributes intelligence data and publishes a daily current events summaries for the President.

Dusan Sokolov Directorate of Economic Intelligence

'I thought an atomic threat would come from the United States, not an environmentalist terror group. Do we have any reliable intelligence on this renegade group?'

'I am sorry Mr President, our intelligence has not provided any information on who this terrorist group is or where they are located,' said Boris Smirnov.

'Do we know if the plutonium stolen from Seversk when it was being decommissioned has been used in these bombs?' asked the president.

'We have no way of knowing sir, however; we do know one kilogram was stolen. That would not be enough to manufacture more than one bomb.'

'I take it that we have no idea how many bombs there are?'

'EDO have intimated they will post in Facebook what cities could be hit and what their specific demands are tomorrow.'

'Yes, via Facebook. No doubt so the whole world will be scared witless.'

'I don't think we can do anything until tomorrow. We will meet again after they publish their demands,' said Ivanov.

ACT NOW
OR
MEET THY DOOM

CHAPTER 12

We have placed atomic bombs in the following cities:
New York
Beijing
Moscow
Berlin
New Delhi
We have already demonstrated to the world our capability.
We demand coal-fired power stations be reduced dramatically to be replaced with clean energy solutions.
OUR DEMANDS ARE:
CHINA
106 NEW COAL POWER STATIONS APPROVED TO CONSTRUCT. CANCEL THEM
130 UNDER CONSTRUCTION CEASE BUILDING
1003 CURRENTLY OPERATING REDUCE BY 40%

INDIA
66 APPROVED FOR CONSTRUCTION CANCEL
41 UNDER CONSTRUCTION CEASE BUILDING
292 CURRENTLY OPERATING REDUCE BY 40%
USA
NONE UNDER CONSTRUCTION
309 OPERATING REDUCE BY 40%
GERMANY
3 UNDER CONSTRUCTION CANCEL
81 OPERATING REDUCE BY 40%
RUSSIA
9 UNDER CONSTRUCTION SEASE BUILDING
78 OPERATING REDUCE BY 40%

If the Goverments of the world don't act now we wi...   Learn More
Your Caption Here

100M   50M Comments   50M Shares

👍 Like   💬 Comment   ➤ Share

President Cooper called Vice President Graham Anderson into the Oval Office. Also present were:

Secretary of State William Morris

Secretary of Defence Michelle Bennett

Secretary of Energy David Murphy

'As you are aware, we have received specific demands from these greenie bastards who can't fucking spell or complete a fucking sentence. We now need to assess if we can achieve their demands before New York disappears.

'David, you're the man responsible for the energy portfolio. Is it possible to agree to their demands?'

'Mr President, we can close the power plants and veto construction of any new ones but without alternatives, pretty well all of America will suffer major blackouts. Of course, that is not only the average citizen missing out on their favourite television programs. It will affect government and industry enormously.'

'So how many wind farms and solar farms will we need to construct?'

'I would have to get the modelling done, but I know it would be at an enormous cost.'

'Replacing New York would be a hell of a lot more. We still don't have any idea where these bastards are located, I take it?'

'The last Facebook posting was using a cell phone. They could be anywhere in the world. Also, they could move to a different location every day,' said Michelle Bennett.

'I'm going to call a video conference with the other heads of government who have been threatened tomorrow. We have to ensure we are all communicating and sharing our intelligence. I want all of you to be present. I'll call Lewis and instruct him to be here.'

'I think that's a positive move Mr President. I think we should also consider getting together industry heads in a conference to discuss how all this will affect them,' said William Morris.

'OK, ask the Secretary of the Treasury to get his department to organise an industry conference as soon as practicable,' said the president.

'I would assume the Secretary General of The United Nations will call for the Security Council to meet as soon as possible also,' said the Secretary of State.

'I'm sure that's true, William, but we can't wait for all the members of the Security Council to fly into New York.'

A video conference was organised for 2 pm the following day. The chairman of the conference was the President of the United States.

In attendance were:

President of the United States, Donald Cooper

President of Russia, Alexander Ivanov

German Chancellor, Helmut Wagner

President of India, Arnav Bakshi

President of China, Fei Hong Zhou

'Gentlemen and Madam President, thank you all for making yourself available for this very important meeting. As you know, a terrorist group calling themselves the Environmental Defence Organisation or EDO have detonated a nuclear bomb in the Pacific as a demonstration to us all as to what they are capable of.'

'Do you think they are bluffing and only ever had the one bomb?' asked Alexander Ivanov.

'That may be the case but are you willing to risk Moscow being the next target if they're not bluffing, Alexander?'

'I see what you mean, Mr President.'

'With all the intelligence resources we have between us all, it's amazing we have virtually zero information about this terrorist group,' said Helmut Wagner.

'Yes, it's very frustrating,' responded President Bakshi.

'I think we need to discuss how we can meet their demands,' said the Madam President of China.

'Yes, I think the Madam President is right. My suggestion is we concentrate on two objectives, tracking down and eliminating EDO and meeting their demands to drastically reduce emissions,' said Donald Cooper. 'Over the next fortnight each country needs to devise a plan to reduce emissions. These plans need to satisfy EDO's demands or at least come very close to it.'

'We should meet again in two weeks via video conference. In the meantime, all our intelligence agencies should be working together to track down these terrorists,' said Lewis Pentecost, Head of the CIA.

'That would make a nice change,' said Helmut Wagner.

FEAR OF FLYING

CHAPTER 13

There was unrest around the globe. The population was demanding that their governments act and act quickly. The demands from EDO had been published on public media, therefore, the peoples of the world knew of the nuclear threat.

Demonstrations in the streets of Berlin, Washington, New Deli, Moscow and Beijing were particularly emotional as these were the cities targeted by EDO. Over one million Chinese marched to Tiananmen Square despite the government prohibiting the demonstration. There were no tanks to suppress the march this time.

Chinese Demonstration

Suva Fiji

Prime Minister Inoke Cakau was pleased with the reaction to EDO's threats and demands. He was also nervous as he was more than aware that every intelligence service was searching for EDO and the terrorists behind it. If Fiji was implicated he and his two ministers would have to take the blame and the subsequent punishment.

His co-conspirators were due for a progress meeting in five minutes.

'Prime Minister, the Defence Minister and the Minister for the Environment are here for your 2 pm meeting,' said Lucy over the intercom.

'Tell them to come in. Lucy could you organise coffee, please?'

The two men entered the Prime Minister's office and the greetings were brief.

'Let's just wait for Lucy to bring in the coffee, then we can begin our briefing.'

The coffee arrived along with some imported Tim Tam biscuits from Australia. They were the Prime Minister's favourites.

'The first issue I would like to discuss is the North Korean scientists. Is it true they have requested Fijian permanent residency?' asked the Prime Minister.

'Yes, they don't wish to return to North Korea,' said George Finau.

'My problem is if we let them stay and a diplomatic row erupts it will bring Fiji to the attention of the UN. There will be questions as to why six North Korean nuclear scientists spent eight months in Fiji. Why was it they departed before completing the project.' said the PM.

'I'm also concerned with the fact that if they do return to North Korea they will crack under pressure and spill the beans as it were,' said Emori.

'So, does anyone have any suggestions?' asked the PM.

'I don't think we can afford a diplomatic rift with North Korea so giving them all residency is not the preferred option as far as I'm concerned,' said George.

'So, what is your preferred option?'

'Well, I hate to say it, but I think they need to be eliminated.'

'Not more assassinations! Don't we have enough blood on our hands already, George?' said Emori.

'OK, what's your solution, Emori?'

'I don't have one but I'm sure there's another way.'

'Well, when you come up with a plan please let me know.'

'Gentlemen, the ultimate decision is mine and I've decided on an appropriate course of action.'

'So, pray what is it, sir?'

'Unfortunately, I have to agree with George. They have to be eliminated. The risk is just too high. We need to orchestrate it to look like an accident so we are above suspicion. I'll leave the details to you, George. Let me know when it's done.'

George had been a lieutenant colonel in the army before entering politics. He was appointed Defence Minister in 2018 after the coup.

He regiment was the SAS "Special Air Services", the elite force in the army.

His experience put him in good stead to develop a plan to take care of the North Korean problem.

Professor Jan Song-Taek was in his hotel room packing his bags. He and his group would be departing Suva for Nadi that morning. The group was extremely disappointed they were not permitted to remain in Fiji. They were then due to board a Fiji Air Boeing 777 for Beijing and then onto Pyongyang. What made it tolerable to return to their draconian homeland was $2,500,000 safely deposited in the Hong Kong Shanghai Bank. The problem they all had was how to access the money when they were stuck in North Korea. That was a problem that could be solved with some imagination and clever manipulation by the bank.

The in-house telephone rang. Jan Song answered it.

'Hello, Jan Song, it's George Finau. How are you? I hope you're packed.'

'Yes, George, I'm ready to go. Would you like me to check on the others?'

'That would be good. I'll call back in fifteen minutes.'

'OK.'

The hotel telephone rang again.

'Well, is everybody ready to go, Jan Song?'

'Yes, George. I suppose there is no chance for a last minute reprieve?'

'I'm afraid not. If it was up to me, maybe but I'm sorry; it's not.

'There's been a slight change of plan. We're going to fly to Nadi. There's been a rock slip over the Suva-Nadi road.'

'I see. Well, it's just another air leg; no problem.'

'You'll be flying by seaplane, taking off from Suva Harbour and landing in Nadi one hour later.'

'That's better than three hours on the road.'

'I'm heading for your hotel now. I'll pick you up and take you to the landing where the seaplane is moored.'

'Excellent.'

George had his driver pull up in front of the lobby area where the North Koreans were waiting with their luggage.

'Right gentlemen, it's only a ten-minute drive.'

The minivan arrived at the landing. None of them had flown in a seaplane before and there was a sense of excitement.

The pilot was David Kama; a very experienced aviator.

The scientists all boarded, did up their seatbelts and waited for the take-off on the water; a totally new experience.

David ensured all the passengers had their seatbelts tightened and then explained a few things about the plane for safety reasons. He then fired up the engines and began taxiing to the designated take-off area.

Once permission was given, he opened the throttle and began moving across the water. The plane picked up speed. The passenger cabin was shaking, then the plane took to the air and there was calm.

The three passengers on the right side of the aircraft could see Suva while those on the left saw the bay.

David had explained that the plane would head for the island of Beqa then head north to Sigatoka and finally across the land to Nadi.

Thirty minutes after take-off, when the aircraft was flying over the Pacific Ocean, David, who was actually an SAS officer, donned his parachute, unlocked the cockpit door and jumped out.

The passengers were appalled at what had happened. As the plane began to nosedive they screamed and cried out but to no avail.

It took five minutes from the time David left the plane until it ploughed into the ocean nose first.

The seaplane broke up on impact and all passengers were killed instantly.

David was picked up by a private launch owned by George Finau and taken back to Suva.

George notified the Prime Minister that the seaplane taking the six North Koreans to Nadi had not arrived.

A search was immediately initiated but they were looking in the wrong area and it was called off after three days.

Weeks later body parts were found on the beach kilometres away from the crash site.

The Fijian Government sent its condolences to the North Korean Government.

A memorial service was held at the Sacred Heart Cathedral but apart from the government cabinet, not many attended.

Sacred Heart Cathedral Suva

MORE DEMANDS

CHAPTER 14

An advertisement was placed in several major newspapers.
The New York Times
China Daily
Southgerman
Pravda Russia
The Times of India

The New York Times

September 2021

EDO has demanded action from the big polluting countries. We also demand action from some of the world's largest corporations who are responsible for 71% of greenhouse gases.

Top 100 producers and their cumulative greenhouse gas emissions from 1988-2015

Count	Company
1	China (Coal)
2	Saudi Arabian Oil Company (Aramco)
3	Gazprom OAO
4	National Iranian Oil Co

Count	Company
5	ExxonMobil Corp
6	Coal India
7	Petroleos Mexicanos (Pemex)
8	Russia (Coal)
9	Royal Dutch Shell PLC
10	China National Petroleum Corp (CNPC)
11	BP PLC
12	Chevron Corp
13	Petroleos de Venezuela SA (PDVSA)
14	Abu Dhabi National Oil Co
15	Poland Coal
16	Peabody Energy Corp
17	Sonatrach SPA
18	Kuwait Petroleum Corp
19	Total SA
20	BHP Billiton Ltd
21	ConocoPhillips
22	Petroleo Brasileiro SA (Petrobras)
23	Lukoil OAO
24	Rio Tinto
25	Nigerian National Petroleum Corp
26	Petroliam Nasional Berhad (Petronas)
27	Rosneft OAO
28	Arch Coal Inc
29	Iraq National Oil Co

Count	Company
30	Eni SPA
31	Anglo American
32	Surgutneftegas OAO
33	Alpha Natural Resources Inc
34	Qatar Petroleum Corp
35	PT Pertamina
36	Kazakhstan Coal
37	Statoil ASA
38	National Oil Corporation of Libya
39	Consol Energy Inc
40	Ukraine Coal
41	RWE AG
42	Oil & Natural Gas Corp Ltd
43	Glencore PLC
44	TurkmenGaz
45	Sasol Ltd
46	Repsol SA
47	Anadarko Petroleum Corp
48	Egyptian General Petroleum Corp
49	Petroleum Development Oman LLC
50	Czech Republic Coal
51	China Petrochemical Corp (Sinopec)
52	China National Offshore Oil Corp Ltd (CNOOC)
53	Ecopetrol SA
54	Singareni Collieries Company

Count	Company
55	Occidental Petroleum Corp
56	Sonangol EP
57	Tatneft OAO
58	North Korea Coal
59	Bumi Resources
60	Suncor Energy Inc
61	Petoro AS
62	Devon Energy Corp
63	Natural Resource Partners LP
64	Marathon Oil Corp
65	Vistra Energy
66	Encana Corp
67	Canadian Natural Resources Ltd
68	Hess Corp
69	Exxaro Resources Ltd
70	YPF SA
71	Apache Corp
72	Murray Coal
73	Alliance Resource Partners LP
74	Syrian Petroleum Co
75	Novatek OAO
76	NACCO Industries Inc
77	KazMunayGas
78	Adaro Energy PT
79	Petroleos del Ecuador

Count	Company
80	Inpex Corp
81	Kiewit Mining Group
82	AP Moller (Maersk)
83	Banpu Public Co Ltd
84	EOG Resources Inc
85	Husky Energy Inc
86	Kideco Jaya Agung PT
87	Bahrain Petroleum Co (BAPCO)
88	Westmoreland Coal Co
89	Cloud Peak Energy Inc
90	Chesapeake Energy Corp
91	Drummond Co
92	Teck Resources Ltd
93	Turkmennebit
94	OMV AG
95	Noble Energy Inc
96	Murphy Oil Corp
97	Berau Coal Energy Tbk PT
98	Bukit Asam (Persero) Tbk PT
99	Indika Energy Tbk PT
100	Southwestern Energy Co

EDO will take action against these companies if they themselves don't take action.

We would like to pay particular attention to BP.

The world was encouraged by BP investing billions of pounds in clean low carbon producing energy throughout the eighties and nineties. For some unknown reason, they have reverted to dirty fossil fuels and abandoned their research into clean energy.

BP was spending over $800 million on research and development alone but now their investment is minuscule.

EDO demands action from BP and other corporations that have abandoned clean energy for the sake of easy profits.

Langley

Lewis Pentecost, the CIA Chief, was under enormous pressure from the President, Congress and the American people. All were demanding answers and he unfortunately didn't have any.

He had operatives scouring the country and the globe searching for these bombs. His people had no idea if the threat was a hoax or if EDO was as powerful as they said they were.

The President was due to chair another video conference the next day. Lewis wasn't looking forward to it.

The President called the Secretary of State, William Morris, and the Secretary of Defence, Michelle Bennett, to the White House and they met in the situation room.

Situation Room

'What the fuck is going on here? We are the most powerful country in the world with the best intelligence and we can't find a few atomic bombs,' said the President.

'We're sorry, Mr President, but it's not that easy. They could be anywhere. The only thing we have to go on is the cities EDO has mentioned in their posts,' said William.

'Not only that, sir; we still know very little about this terrorist group. They use social media to make their demands and now they're placing ads in the major newspapers. We don't know who their leader is or how many terrorists in the organisation. At least with TMA the leader, Abdel Bakr al-Baghda, is known to the world.'

'Why are the newspapers permitting these ads to be printed?' asked the President.

'They figure it's better for the population to be informed rather than wake up one day with an atomic bomb exploding in their living room,' said Michelle.

'Well, they wouldn't fucking wake up would they?'

'I was talking metaphorically, sir.'

'OK, I wanted to talk to you two first before Lewis joins us. He's due round about now.'

The intercom buzzed, and Lewis Pentecost was announced by one of the marines guarding the President.

'Send him in please.'

'Hello, Lewis, we're looking forward to your briefing. What has the CIA discovered about this EDO group?'

'I'm afraid not a lot; we are pursuing an investigation into the mysterious disappearance of the salvage vessel *Aurarius* in the Pacific near Fiji.'

'What's that got to do with anything?'

'Sir, there was an incident involving a Skyhawk attached to the *USS Ticonderoga* in December 1966. The fighter jet fell off the ship's plane lift and disappeared in 14,000 feet of water carrying the pilot and two atomic bombs.'

'I take it these broken arrows have never been found?'

'No sir.'

'The salvage ship the *Aurarius* was owned by the billionaire, Richard Manson. He was searching for the *Vanderbilt*, which was sunk by the Japanese in 1943. It is reputed to be carrying $1,000,000,000 in gold bullion to Australia obviously a lot more than that in today's prices.'

'OK, it's getting more interesting; continue.'

'Richard Manson was run over by a fast-moving SUV while taking his daily walk in New York. He died instantly.'

'So, you think there may be a connection to these incidents?'

'We're not sure but we are pursuing it.'

'Anything else?'

'Fiji seconded six nuclear scientists from North Korea to design a nuclear power station at the beginning of this year. They all were killed in a light plane crash. This may be just a coincidence but it's worth pursuing.'

'Why was Fiji dealing with North fucking Korea of all countries to build a nuclear reactor? There are plenty of other countries that could have helped them build it, including us. I think it is worth pursuing,

Lewis. I'm suspicious of anything to do with North Korea. How many operatives do we have on the ground in Fiji at the moment?'

'Four, sir.'

'I want you to double it. We need to know if EDO is based there although my gut says no.'

PEOPLE POWER

CHAPTER 15

EDO sent out a message via social media, insisting the people of the world must begin driving clean electric and hydrogen cars.

'EDO will ensure new car purchases will follow the Norwegian model. No sales tax, no registration fee and free parking.'

Motor vehicles, planes and ships contribute approximately 15% of man-made carbon dioxide.

By eliminating the majority of coal-fired power stations and converting to electric cars, EDO will be satisfied with the progress being made but there is much more to be done.

There is more we can do to save the planet. postings soon.'

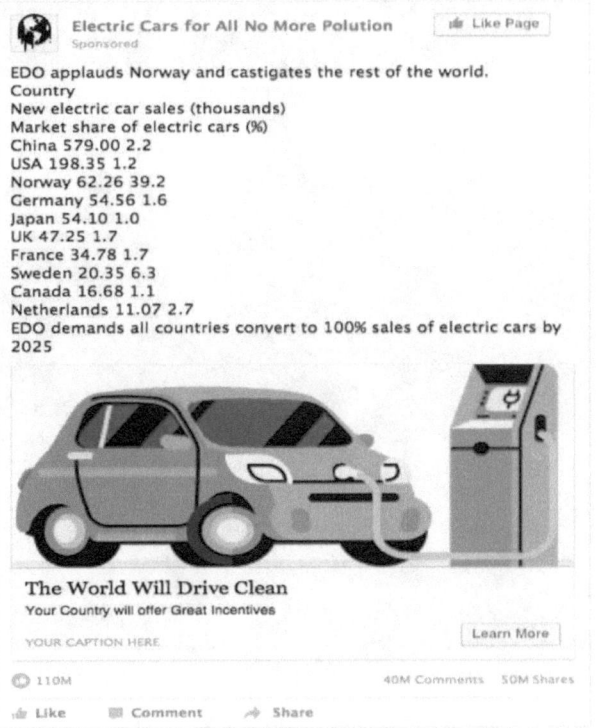

Electric Cars for All No More Polution
Sponsored
Like Page

EDO applauds Norway and castigates the rest of the world.
Country
New electric car sales (thousands)
Market share of electric cars (%)
China 579.00 2.2
USA 198.35 1.2
Norway 62.26 39.2
Germany 54.56 1.6
Japan 54.10 1.0
UK 47.25 1.7
France 34.78 1.7
Sweden 20.35 6.3
Canada 16.68 1.1
Netherlands 11.07 2.7
EDO demands all countries convert to 100% sales of electric cars by 2025

The World Will Drive Clean
Your Country will offer Great Incentives

YOUR CAPTION HERE
Learn More

110M
40M Comments 50M Shares

Like   Comment   Share

People around the world were terrified that an atomic bomb could be detonated in their city; they were also terrified of what global warming could do to the planet.

Demonstrations took place in every major city. Governments could not ignore people power. They insisted their leaders accelerate their efforts to adhere to EDO's demands. It wasn't just the fear of a nuclear explosion in their cities that motivated them; they believed the EDO's environmental plans were justified.

Washington

Moscow

Beijing

London

Berlin

New Delhi

DECEPTION

CHAPTER 16

Washington D.C.

Another video conference was arranged to discuss the situation, attending were:

President of the United States, Donald Cooper
President of Russia, Alexander Ivanov
German Chancellor, Helmut Wagner
President of India, Arnav Bakshi
President of China, Mrs Fei Hong Zhou
Prime Minister of Great Britain, Geoffrey Baird.

'Welcome Madam President and gentlemen, I have invited Prime Minister Baird to join us as although Britain has not been directly threatened they have more than just a passing interest. As you are all aware we have received more demands from EDO and their threats are getting more severe. I assume their intelligence is sophisticated, hence they probably know of this video hook-up. Today I think each of us should report on our progress re their demands,' said Donald Cooper.

'I would like to be first to report on our progress,' said Alexander Ivanov.

'Firstly I think we are all aware we can't just shut down the majority of our coal-fired power stations as it would create chaos. We need time to build alternative energy facilities. I suggest we use social media to ask for a reasonable extension of time.'

'Terrorists don't see reason, Alexander,' said Donald Cooper.

'But closing down thirty-one power stations and cancelling the construction of another nine will bring my country to its knees.'

'That's why we need to hunt them down,' said the Chinese President.

'I agree with Alexander. I think we should request an extension, however, at the same time, we should devote the majority of our intelligence agencies to seeking these bastards out,' said Helmut Wagner.

'Is everybody here in agreement?' asked Donald Cooper.

All present nodded agreement.

'What's our plan B if they refuse our request?' said Arnav Bakshi.

'Why don't we place the posting and see what sort of reaction we get? If it's negative we will need to devise a plan B,' said Cooper.

'Do you think we should communicate with them under the banner of the United Nations?' asked Alexander Ivanov.

'Yes, I think that would be the right thing to do. Does everybody agree?'

The agreement was made amongst the major nations.

A Message to the Leaders of EDO
Sponsored
Like Page

The leaders of the following nations:
President of the United States Donald Cooper
President of Russia Alexander Ivanov
German Chancellor Helmut Wagner
President of India Arnav Bakshi
President of China Mrs Fei Hong Zhou
Prime Minister of Great Britain Geoffrey Baird.
Acknowledge the need to reduce CO2 in the earth's atmosphere and are endeavouring to meet EDO's timetable, however, we ask that more time is given to reach your very ambitious goals. We assure EDO that there demands will be met.

The Nations of the Planet are Committed to a Clean Earth
EDO we agree to your demads but need more time

CLEAN EARTH
Learn More

50K
14K Comments   10K Shares

Like   Comment   Share

Donald Cooper read the post. 'Bloody hell we accuse these pricks of not being able to spell and we are just as bad as them. Who proofed this post?'

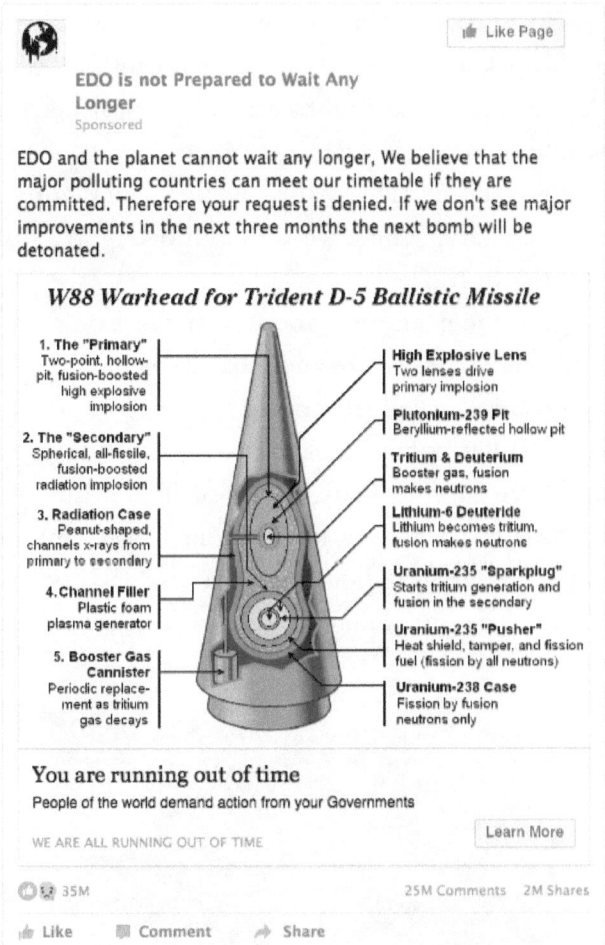

Suva Fiji

Inoke Cakau, Prime Minister of Fiji, and his two partners were meeting to discuss their next move.

'Well, Prime Minister, we have certainly stirred up a hornets' nest around the world,' said George Finau, the Defence Minister.

'Yes, we have. I hope it will all be worth it. I know the CIA are sniffing around Fiji at the moment and I'm sure MI5 and the others are doing the same.'

'I thought our tracks were well and truly covered. I'm sure they won't find anything,' said Emori, the Minister for the Environment.

'Don't forget we killed several Americans, sank an American ship and stole two American nuclear bombs all within Fijian territorial waters. Of course we would be on their radar.'

'Do you think we should lay low for a while?' said George.

'No, quite the contrary; I think we should move it up a notch.'

'What do you mean, Inoke?'

'I think we give them another month. If we don't see significant change we remind them who we are and what we want.'

'How do we do that?' asked Emori.

'We detonate another bomb,' replied the Prime Minister.

'But we don't have a bomb spare. They are all in position.'

'Then we detonate one that is in position. I don't mean blow up a city. I'm suggesting we take the bomb in Moscow and transport it up to the tundra in Siberia. The only thing we kill is a few reindeer and a couple of rabbits.'

Siberian Tundra

'That sounds like a plan; it should scare the shit out of them all.'

'How do you think we should handle the CIA and MI5 etc. when they start asking questions?' asked George.

'Just remember the only people that know anything about EDO are in this room. They can ask all the questions they like. They won't get the answers they're looking for.'

'What about David? He must know, having murdered the North Koreans.'

'I'm afraid David is no longer with us.'

'You didn't.'

'I had to, Emori. We can't take any chances. Think of the big picture.'

'I've said it before. I hope it's worth it.'

AS COLD AS THE ICE ON THE TUNDRA

CHAPTER 17

Suva Fiji

The three members of EDO began planning the Russian operation. They gave it the code name Rasputin. One conundrum was the logistics of how to transport the bomb to a completely isolated area, which probably didn't have roads.

'I have an idea,' said Inoke.

'What is it?' asked George.

'I read an article about a new drone that can carry heavy payloads. Not only that, but it can be operated from a significant distance. I suggest we attach the bomb to the drone and fly it to a completely deserted area and detonate it via mobile phone.'

'That sounds like it could work. What's the name of this drone?'

'It's called the Griff 300. It can lift 300 kilograms, which is amazing.'

'We need to set up a bogus account so that the drone can't be traced back to us,' said Inoke.

'Don't worry, I can organise the purchase. Rest assured, the CIA will not be able to trace it,' said George.

'Do we know how much this thing costs?' asked Inoke.

'They're not cheap. I think I read about $250,000.'

'Shit, they're not cheap are they?'

'No they're not; especially when you think what will be left of it after the blast.'

'Nothing much will be left after the blast for a good ten kilometre radius,' George said drily.

Griff 300

'I'll leave it up to you two to work out the logistics. I'd like you to come back to me next week.'

'Yes sir. We'll do our best.'

'You'll have to. We need this to work.'

George Finau had the resources of the Fijian army available to him, but this operation was top secret. He couldn't just enter the officers' mess and explain the operation and request a volunteer.

He knew of one particular soldier whose name was Kabu Vula; a captain in the 1ˢᵗ Battalion who had served in Afghanistan as part of the Fijian peacekeeping force. He was known for his bravery and his intelligence; two attributes George was looking for in an operative.

George arranged to meet him at the Fijian Resort, near Nadi; away from prying eyes in Suva.

The Fijian Resort

George booked a suite at the resort where the meeting would take place.

Kabu used his mobile phone to call George to inform his commander in chief that he was in the lobby. George gave him the room number.

Five minutes later there was a knock on the door. George opened it and greeted the soldier warmly.

'It's good to see you, Kabu; it has been some time.'

'Yes, sir, not since I returned from Afghanistan.'

'Good heavens, when was that?'

'Late 2014.'

'Well, time flies doesn't it Kabu?'

'It does, sir.'

'What have you been up to? Are you married?'

'Yes, sir, I've been married for six years. My wife Mila is six months pregnant.'

'Congratulations to you both. I suppose you have her wrapped up in cottonwool?'

'You don't know Mila, sir. She's a keen sailor and she's probably sailing while I'm away.'

'Well, you tell her to be careful; that's precious cargo she's carrying. Kids are wonderful. I have two boys and two girls and they keep me grounded.

'Right, down to business. You're probably wondering why I wanted to meet with you and why all the cloak and dagger.'

'I'd have to say it has crossed my mind, sir.'

'Kabu, what I am about to tell you is absolutely top secret. If you divulge any of this information it will cost you your life. Do you understand?'

'I'm not sure I want to hear what you have to say, sir.'

'That's a choice only you can make, however, I'm giving you the chance to make an enormous contribution to the future safety of your country.'

'Seeing you put it like that, sir, what is it you wish to tell me?'

George briefed the young captain on EDO but he excluded the assassinations of the Americans and North Koreans.

'I'm a patriot as you well know, sir, and I too am worried about Fiji's future; therefore, I am willing to accept the assignment.'

'I knew I could rely on you, Kabu.'

'When do I leave and when do I get briefed as to where exactly I'm going?'

'I would expect you to leave in a fortnight.'

'How long should I expect to be away sir?'

'No more than a month.'

'And the destination?'

'All in good time, Captain.'

'I just need to let my family know.'

'Kabu, remember you mustn't tell anyone; not even your wife.'

'I understand, sir.'

'Well, I think we should retire to the restaurant. I'm famished. I have booked you a room for tonight rather than driving back to Suva.'

'Thank you, sir, I'll let my wife know.'

The two Fijians met again at breakfast, which was delivered to George's suite.

'Sir, I've been thinking. I will need diplomatic status to ensure I'm not stopped and searched.'

'Yes, I will arrange for your papers to be drawn up. By the way, you can call me George.'

'Well, George, I officially accept the assignment.'

'Excellent. Fiji appreciates your commitment and dedication.'

Kabu drove back to Suva after breakfast. He wasn't due back at the barracks until the following day.

HEARTBREAK

CHAPTER 18

The young captain drove up the driveway and parked the SUV in the garage.

Kabu and Mila lived in one of Suva's better suburbs, Samabula. It was close to the water, which suited Mila.

The young army captain was feeling a little weary for it had been an intensive couple of days. He grabbed a cold Fiji Draught from the fridge and sat in his recliner. He hoped Mila would be home soon as he had lots to discuss with her. It wasn't long before he fell asleep.

The doorbell woke him. Kabu reluctantly opened the front door. Standing in front of him were two police officers; one male and one female.

The female officer said, 'Captain Vula?'

'Yes, that's me. What can I do for you?'

'May we come inside, Captain? We need to talk to you.'

'What's wrong?'

'If we could just come inside, Captain.'

'OK, but I haven't done anything wrong, I can assure you.'

'We know you haven't, sir.'

'Well, come into the lounge room. Can I get you a Fiji Water or a Coke or something?'

'No thanks, we're fine. Captain Vula, we have some very sad news for you.'

'What?'

'Your wife was drowned in a boating accident.'

'No, that's bullshit. She's a great swimmer. She couldn't possibly drown.'

'We are so sorry, Captain. We understand it's a double tragedy as she was pregnant.'

'With tears running down his face Kabu managed to ask where she was and if he could see her.

'She is in the morgue, sir. You need to identify her. I know now is not a good time but may we suggest 10 am tomorrow?'

'Yes, I suppose so. How did this possibly happen?

'I believe an enquiry will be held. Hopefully some answers will come from that.'

'OK, may I ask you to leave? I need some time alone.'

'Yes, of course, Captain. Our sympathy is with you.'

The two police officers left the house.

Back in the police vehicle, the female police officer said, 'This is the worst part of the job. I hate it. It makes me feel like the grim reaper.'

'Yeah, I know what you mean,' said Constable Mara.

Kabu sat down in his favourite chair once again and sobbed uncontrollably for an hour. He felt totally drained, empty and lonely.

He lifted himself out of the recliner and went into the bedroom where there were several photos of him and Mila smiling and in love on the dresser. He threw himself down on the bed and sobbed again for what seemed like an eternity.

Finally, he fell asleep fully clothed, but he woke many times throughout the night and each time he woke reality hit him. He knew he wasn't dreaming.

The next morning Kabu telephoned his sister Elizabeth and informed her of Mila's demise. She too was distraught. They arranged to meet that afternoon to discuss the funeral arrangements.

Kabu showered and dressed, but he neither shaved or ate breakfast. He drove to the yacht club where Mila had been an active member. He sat on a bench seat overlooking the harbour; the same harbour where his one true love had lost her life.

He looked at his watch. It was 9.30 am; time to go and identify Mila.

Kabu arrived at the Suva Morgue five minutes early. He opened the glove box and took out a packet of Benson & Hedges. He had given up smoking when he learned of Mila's pregnancy but had kept this packet in case of emergencies.

Smoking somehow calmed him down and gave him strength for what he was about to do.

At 10 am he locked the car and entered the building where he approached the receptionist and introduced himself.

'Please take a seat, Captain Vula. Someone will be with you shortly.'

After five minutes, a gentleman approached. He wasn't wearing a white coat as Kabu was expecting.

'Hello, Captain Vula, my name is John Tuwai. Please accept my condolences for your great loss.'

'Thank you.'

'Captain, I know this will be difficult for you but by law, you must identify your wife.'

'I understand.'

'Follow me, sir.'

Kabu followed the coroner down a long sparkling clean linoleum hallway.

He indicated to Kabu that the next door on the left would be where they would enter.

Kabu observed stainless steel doors three rows high and running down about twenty metres.

The coroner asked Kabu if he was ready.

He just nodded.

John pulled out the drawer and Kabu gasped. Lying in this stainless steel cold drawer was the love of his life. He just stared, with tears rolling down his cheeks.

'Captain, I must ask you to identify her. Is this Mila Vula, your wife?'

Kabu couldn't speak.

'Kabu, I must ask you to verbally indicate if this person is your wife.'

'Yes.'

'Thank you sir, I know it's been very hard for you. You will be able to view her again at the funeral home.'

The coroner slid the drawer shut, but Kabu could not move.

'Captain Vula, it's time to go. I will escort you out.'

Kabu was in a daze. He couldn't remember leaving the morgue and driving home and it was only when he raised the garage door that he realised he was home. Or was it home anymore?

Kabu's sister Elizabeth organised the funeral. It was held in Sacred Heart, the same cathedral as the North Koreans' had been; the difference being that Mila had two-hundred mourners while the former had twenty-five.

WINGS

CHAPTER 19

Captain Vula returned to barracks two weeks after the funeral. His first meeting was with the Defence Minister George Finau.

'Firstly, may I offer my condolences. What a tragedy.'

'Thank you, sir, I appreciated the flowers you and your wife sent to the house. They were beautiful.'

'That was the least we could do. It was our intention to attend the funeral, but I was called away on urgent business.'

'I understand, sir.'

'Kabu, remember what I said; call me George in private.'

'Yes, sorry George.'

'Now Kabu, I'm afraid we need to talk business. Are you up to it?'

'Yes, I am. I'm looking forward to the assignment. It will take my mind off recent events.'

'Good, you will be leaving on December 20th, that's Friday week. All the paperwork is in order, including your diplomatic status.'

'Excellent, but you still haven't told me where I'm going, George.'

'You will be fully briefed all in good time. Don't worry, we're not sending you to Antarctica.'

Not far off it though, George thought.

'You will need to train on a specific piece of equipment. It's top secret, and therefore we need to train you in an isolated location. A Jeep will pick you up tomorrow at 5 am.'

'Yes sir, thank you, George.'

Kabu wondered what the equipment was that required such intensive training. He was proficient in firing all the weapons used by the Fijian military.

He set the alarm on his iPhone to wake him at 4 am. He then watched some television and went to bed.

The irritating alarm sounded right on time. He got out of bed, showered and dressed. Even though Fiji had a tropical climate, it was quite cold at this time of morning. He carried a coat in case he needed it.

Kabu waited until he heard a car horn. It was the Jeep and presumably the person that would train him on the mysterious piece of equipment.

Kabu locked the front door and walked down to the street where he eased himself into the vehicle.

'Good morning Captain Vula. My name is Corporal Timi Leba. I will be training you today.'

'I'm pleased to meet you. Training me in what, exactly?'

'I was instructed not to tell you, sir, until we reach the practice site.'

'This is getting to be a little ridiculous I'll be seeing the whatever it is soon anyway. I'm your superior officer and I order you to tell me.'

I'm sorry sir, but my orders come from a higher rank.'

'Right.'

The Jeep reached its destination ten minutes later at a vast field, completely flat and devoid of trees.

'Sir, would you help lift the box out of the back?'

'Whatever this secret machine is it's bloody heavy.'

Timi and Kabu lifted the machine out of the box and placed it on the grass. Kabu still didn't have a clue what this thing was; it was only when Timi unfolded the rotor arms, all eight of them, that it became clear to Kabu it was a very large drone.

He now knew what this training was all about. This drone would carry the bomb.

'OK, Captain, I'll start her up and fly her around. You stand beside me and watch how I use the controls. It's quite simple really.'

It looked simple and after a few heavy landings Kabu started to get the hang of it.

Griff 300 Control Unit

By the end of the day, the rookie had become proficient in flying the $250,000 drone.

He also learnt that he could control the Griff from twenty kilometres away, which would place him in a safe zone when the device was detonated.

The two men packed the drone into its box and drove back to Suva. Both of them felt it had been a worthwhile exercise.

When Timi reported back to the Minister of Defence, he gave Kabu a high pass. George was delighted as flying the drone was an integral part of the plan.

The planned date for the detonation was January 1, 2022, at the following times.

Suva 10 am January 1
Moscow Midnight January 1
Washington DC 4 pm December 31
Berlin 10 pm 31 December
New Delhi 2.30 am January 1
Beijing 5 am January 1

The bomb would be detonated by the Prime Minister's satellite phone, using a code only he knew.

The time had arrived when Kabu was to be informed of his destination. George called him, requesting his presence.

'Hello, Kabu please take a seat. Can I get you anything?'

'No thank you George, I'm eager to discover where you're sending me.'

'Yes, I imagine you are. I'm afraid it's nowhere exotic. Here is your Emirates business class ticket.'

Kabu took the ticket, examining his destination. You're going to blow up Moscow!'

'No, Kabu. Once you arrive in Moscow, you pick up a hire car; a Mercedes 4WD, and drive to our embassy at 14A/2 Podkolokolny Pereulok.

'There you will pick up the suitcase and the crate with the Griff drone.

'You will then return to the airport where you will catch a plane to Novosibirsk, Siberia. Another hire car will be waiting for you at the airport; the same model as in Moscow.

'You will then be driving north for two days. I will give you the GPS coordinates and your car is equipped with satellite navigation. I'm afraid you'll need to sleep in the 4WD, as there are no Airbnbs out there. A sleeping bag and doona is provided.

'Once you have reached:

Longitude: 99.196656

Latitude: 61.013710,

you are at ground zero. Leave the Griff and go back at least twenty kilometres. Fifteen minutes before detonation time raise the Griff one hundred metres above ground level and keep it hovering.

'When you hear the blast, drive back to Novosibirsk and then onto Moscow and then home.'

'What if I'm stopped at the airport?'

'You claim diplomatic immunity.'

As Kabu drove home to his empty lifeless house he started to think about his future. He suspected George had organised the plane to crash with the North Koreans on board. He also suspected that George murdered his good friend David for some reason unknown. Would he be next? Did he know too much?

He was due to fly out to Moscow in the morning and he needed a good night's sleep. There would be plenty of time to think on the twenty-hour flight.

LESE-MAJESTE

CHAPTER 20

Suva Fiji

4 am

Kabu rang his good friend in Afghanistan; Ashtak Karzai. The two men had established a strong bond when the Fijian captain had been posted to Kabul.

The essence of the conversation related around the political stability in the country and the dominance of the Taliban forces over the Afghani army. Kabu had long suspected his friend supported the Taliban.

Kabu intimated he might be able to visit his good friend at the end of his official business in Moscow. It was agreed that Kabu would call him if he was able to make it.

Kabu dressed in his uniform, ate breakfast and waited for the taxi to take him to Suva Airport. At 8 am he heard the taxi beep its horn. He grabbed his bag and locked the door behind him.

Once he boarded the Boing 777 he closed his eyes. The plane hadn't even begun to taxi when he fell asleep.

He woke up when the flight attendants were wheeling the drinks trolley through business class. He chose a whisky and began to think again about his future.

By the time the plane reached Moscow, he had a clear plan.

He went to the Hertz desk and picked up his Mercedes. With the aid of his satellite navigation, he located the Fijian embassy. Moscow traffic was even worse than Suva's.

He asked to see the ambassador and he was directed to her anteroom where he waited for twenty minutes. Finally, she came out of her office and introduced herself.

110

'Hello, I am Margaret Dawai. Please come into my office. I'm sorry to have kept you waiting… urgent business I'm afraid.'

'I understand ma'am.'

'So, I believe we have been holding a diplomatic suitcase and a crate for you?'

'Yes, that's correct. I was wondering if I could collect them now. I'm on a tight timetable.'

'But I understand you only arrived in Moscow a few hours ago?'

'Yes ma'am, but I have to catch a plane up north.'

'That's a shame. You won't see Moscow; it's a beautiful city.'

'I'll hope I'll get to see it when I return.'

'I hope you do; I'll get somebody to help you carry them to your car.'

'Thank you, ma'am.'

Once the two items were safely in the back of the Mercedes the young captain drove to the airport. He purchased a ticket to Kabul, Afghanistan.

On arrival in Kabul he called Ashtak and he asked his good friend to arrange a meeting with a very important Afghani dignitary.

'Kabu, that's like asking an English friend to set up a meeting with the Queen.'

'Do your best, old friend; it's important.'

'I'll see what I can do. Can I tell him the purpose of the meeting?'

'Just tell him I have a solution to end the war within a week in the Taliban's favour.'

'That's a bold claim. I'll get back to you.'

'Tell him time is of the essence.'

Suva

December 21

Inoke Cakau was sitting at his desk in the Prime Minister's office. He would soon be joined by his co-conspirators.

'The Defence Minister and the Minister for the Environment are here to see you, sir.'

'Thank you Lucy, please show them in.'

'Good morning, Prime Minister.'

'Good morning, gentlemen; please sit down. As you are both aware we are about to demonstrate to the major powers that we are very serious about our demands. I know you are both keen to know when and where the detonation will take place. I can now divulge the details to you both.

'We discussed Siberia some time ago and I can now confirm the bomb will be detonated in northern Siberia on January 1.'

'Inoke, can you describe the logistics? How will the bomb get to the blast position?'

'It's best you are not aware of all fine details Emori; however, we will be using the Griff 300 as you suggested.'

'If this second explosion doesn't motivate these politicians we have no choice but to detonate the third bomb over a major city,' said Inoke.

'Please God don't let it come to that,' said George.

'Don't worry, George they will listen to us this time,' said Inoke.

Kabul, Afghanistan

December 21

Kabu approached the luggage counter. As his luggage was labelled diplomatic it didn't come out on the carousel with the other luggage.

He signed the release form and used a trolley to transfer his deadly cargo to a secure baggage locker.

Ashtak was waiting to greet him in the terminal.

'Hello, my old friend, how's my Fijian warrior?'

'I'm not sure about warrior. It's good to see you again Ashtak, my friend.'

'Why don't we have a coffee and I can bring you up to date.'

'Great, I'm looking forward to hearing your news.'

The two men walked to the end of the passenger terminal where a coffee shop was located.

They ordered coffee and sat a far table.

'You're not going to believe it, but he is willing to meet with you. Your statement about the Taliban winning the war in a week got him interested.'

'Excellent. When can I see him?'

'Tomorrow.'

'OK, that's good. I am on a very strict timeline.'

'Kabu, can you tell me what your plan is?'

'I'm sorry, dear friend, I can't. You're going to have to trust me. Do you have instructions for me?'

'Yes, you need to hire a Land Cruiser. Ask them for white armour-plated vehicle.

'You are to drive to the outskirts of Kabul and park at Sarab Gas Station.

'Someone will meet you there; follow their instructions.'

TALIBAN

CHAPTER 21

Sarab Gas Station

Kabu waited for over an hour. He was beginning to think the meeting was cancelled.

He looked down the road and saw three Prados approaching. They pulled up in the gas station. One man got out and walked over to Kabu's vehicle. He had a submachine gun under his right arm.

'Are you Kabu?'

'I am.'

'Get out of the car and come with me.'

'I don't wish to leave my car here. Can I follow you?'

'No you can't; lock it and come with me.'

Kabu knew it would be futile to argue and possibly even dangerous. Once in the back of the Prado, he was blindfolded. They drove for what Kabu estimated about an hour before stopping. His blindfold remained in place as they guided the Fijian captain into some sort of room.

'Sit down.' A hand guided the blindfolded man down to what felt like a large cushion.

He sat in this position for what seemed an age but in fact was only twenty minutes. Finally, the blindfold was removed.

Sitting in front of him was a very distinguished man; Mullah Hibatullah Akhundzada.

Mullah Hibatullah Akhundzada

Once the blindfold was removed the hospitality improved.

'Mr Kabu can I offer you a cup of tea or some other refreshment?'

'I would like a glass of water if that is possible, Mullah.'

'Now, you mentioned on the phone that you had something in your possession which you thought my organisation would be very keen to purchase. Is that correct?'

'Yes, that's correct.'

'It's not an aircraft carrier, is it? We would have little use for one in Afghanistan,' he joked.

'No Mullah, it is a very sophisticated one megaton nuclear bomb.'

Mullah Hibatullah Akhundzada just stared at Kabu; not a word was spoken for a minute.

'Mr Kabu, Afghanistan is a complex country fighting a complex war. There is no one centre, no front where an enemy can be targeted. Taliban mix with the general population in all our cities. So, you see such a device would not be practical here. You would be better off speaking to our brothers in TMA.'

'Yes, I can see your point, but one thing I didn't mention was this device will be detonated on January 1, and therefore, there is not much time. Is there any way you can introduce me to the TMA leadership?'

'I may be able to. Leave it with me. What hotel are you staying in?'

'The Intercontinental.'

116

'I'll have someone reach you there with the contact details.'

'Thank you, Mullah.'

'Just as a matter of interest… what do you propose to charge for your bomb?'

'$25,000,000.'

'That's a lot of money; good luck getting it.'

'Plutonium is near impossible to obtain plus the bomb was built by experts so it's not a dirty bomb. I believe it to be a fair price.'

'Return to your hotel. I will endeavour to contact the leader of the TMA to set up a meeting.'

Thank you Mullah. I'd just like to reiterate; the bomb will be detonated on January 1. I have no control over it therefore if we don't act quickly it could be detonated in Kabul.'

'We have ways to encourage you to disclose the location of the bomb.'

'I'm sure it won't come to that although if it does we have fail-safe procedures in place. Goodbye Mullah.'

Kabu returned to the Intercontinental where he selected a small bottle of Chivas Regal from the mini bar. Sitting down in the club chair sipping his scotch and ice, he contemplated his next move.

Situation Room White House Washington

The President of the United States was in a dilemma. With him were Secretary of State William Morris and Secretary of Defence Michelle Bennett.

'We know this EDO terrorist group are going to detonate another bomb and we know it will be in Siberia where it can't do any real harm. What we don't know is will they explode the next one in a major city as they are threatening to do,' said President Cooper.

'Sir, after the Pacific blast we were sceptical as to whether they had another bomb to explode. If in fact the Siberian explosion happens as they say it will on January 1, I think we can assume they have more,' said Michelle Bennett.

'What worries me the most is how they acquired these bombs. Iran would have to be high on the list,' said William Morris.

'How many coal-fired power stations have we retired in the past three months?'

'I believe it is five, sir. We can't build alternative energy sources quickly enough. If we simply close down more, half of the USA will suffer severe blackouts,' said Morris.

'Do you think this EDO rabble will think that's fast enough? Surely they can see we are trying to meet their demands,' said President Cooper.

'Another demand as you know is all new motor vehicle sales will be electric or hydrogen. How's that going?'

'We are talking to the big car manufacturers as well as Tesla. They are baulking at the rate of change except for Tesla of course,' said Morris.

'Fuck them! They'd better get on board or I will nationalise them.'

'Well let's see what they come back with,' said Michelle.

'Can you arrange the cabinet to be in the Situation Room on January 1, William, so we can all view the show?'

'Yes, Mr President.'

Moscow War Room

Alexander Ivanov, the President of Russia, had called his war cabinet together to discuss the latest developments with EDO.

'So apparently the next nuclear detonation will be in Siberia on January 1. The GPS coordinates they have given us indicate it will be detonated in a remote region.'

'At least no one will be hurt,' said Boris Smirnov of Counterintelligence.

'Boris, what has your department discovered about this EDO group?'

'I'm afraid we haven't discovered anything yet. It's not for a lack of trying, Mr President.'

'We are supposed to have the preeminent spy organisation in the world yet you can't even tell me where these bastards are located.'

'We'll keep trying Mr President. We will leave no stone unturned.'

Yes, I'm sure you won't. What's happening with the retirement of the power stations?'

'We have closed four so far all in the south of the country,' said Egor Kuznetsov.

'Why not in the north?' asked the President.

'It's almost impossible to replace coal as solar power wouldn't generate enough power. There's not enough sun.'

'What about wind power?'

'We're looking into it.'

'Well you better get a hurry on or we will all be vaporised.'

Chancellor's Office Berlin Germany

Karl Weber was sitting in his normal place at the centre of the cabinet table, surrounded by his cabinet colleagues.

'You are all aware that a second atomic bomb will be detonated in a few days in Siberia, Russia. EDO have claimed that if they don't see significant progress the next bomb will be detonated in a major city, possibly Berlin.

'So, where are we at as far as satisfying their demands?'

'We have retired six coal powered power stations and cancelled six from being built,' said Helmut Schmidt, the Energy Minister.

'We need to find out if they are satisfied with our progress,' said Weber.

'That's hard to do considering we have no idea who they are and where they are located, Chancellor.'

'That's true. What about electric and hydrogen cars?'

'All our major car manufacturers are committed to electric vehicles. They're slower manufacturing hydrogen cars but they are making progress.'

'We made a commitment to install 1000 EV Charging stations throughout Germany. To date we have installed three hundred,' said Helmut Schmidt.

1000 EV Charging stations

'They must see we are trying to satisfy their demands, surely,' said Karl Weber.

Beijing, China

The President of China was Fei Hong Zhou, a very powerful woman who was admired by a vast majority of the people.

Her conundrum was how to reduce the number of power stations down from 1003 to a number which would be acceptable to EDO. They had specified 40% reduction; however, she knew that would be an impossible target to meet in the short term.

She was frustrated that she had no way of negotiating with these people other than posting a response on Facebook.

Fei Hong Zhou was confident that EDO would be satisfied with the number of electric cars now registered although China had 300,000,000 petrol and diesel cars on the road, which was more than the USA. In Mao's time it was rare to see a car on the road at all as cycles were the preferred mode of transportation.

TMA

CHAPTER 22

The Intercontinental Hotel

Kabu decided to go downstairs to the restaurant. He hadn't eaten a decent meal in days. He ordered fillet mignon and a glass of French red wine. He enjoyed the first glass so much he ordered another.

After dinner, he returned to his room and picked up the remote. The only program he could find was CNN. He watched the world news for an hour and went to bed.

At 3 am two hooded men holding AK47s shook him awake. They were standing at his bedside demanding he get out of bed, dress and come with them. He didn't need much convincing but did as he was told.

They used the service lift to descend to the basement where another hooded man was seated behind the wheel of a black Land Cruiser. The two men pushed Kabu into the back seat and told him to keep down. One of the men tied a blindfold around his head. Kabu began to think this was the norm for travelling in Afghanistan.

The Fijian estimated the journey took two hours but finally, they arrived at their destination. He was rough-handled out of the 4WD and dragged, still blindfolded, into a building where he was instructed to sit.

Five minutes later he heard voices. He had no idea what they were saying. The blindfold was removed and once he adjusted to the light he was confronted with six hooded TMA terrorists all carrying submachine guns.

In walked the leader of TMA, Abu Bakr al-Baghdadi. All six terrorists bowed their heads and Kabu thought it prudent to do the same.

Abu Bakr al-Baghdadi

'So why was it so urgent to see me?'
'I have an atomic bomb which you may be interested in.'
'How did you get this bomb?'
'I'm afraid I can't tell you.'
'How many kilotons?'
'It's actually one megaton.'
'Is it a plutonium bomb?'
'Yes, it is; hence it only weighs twenty-three kilos.'
'Is it in Afghanistan?'
'Yes.'
'I assume you want a lot of money for this bomb.'
'I want $25,000,000.'

'I see. What's to stop us torturing you until you tell us where the bomb is located?'

'The bomb will be detonated by a timer attached to the device. It is in a metal suitcase with two combinations. I know one of the combinations but not the other.'

'Who knows the other?'

'An organisation on the other side of the world. Their leader, whom I have never met, is the only one who can, together with me, change the detonation time or disarm the bomb. The case has a camera so only I can unlock my combination once I'm identified. If the case is broken into the bomb will detonate.

'I must tell you the bomb will be detonated at 1.30 am on the 1st of January Afghani time.'

'Why then?'

'The bomb was due to be detonated in Siberia at that time to warn world leaders they must act on climate change.'

'Ah, so you are connected with EDO the organisation that detonated a nuclear bomb in the Pacific?'

'That's right, except I decided to go out on my own as it were.'

'So the leader of EDO believes he will be detonating his bomb in Siberia?'

'That's correct; hence the January 1 deadline.'

'I will call together my cabinet and discuss our options. You are fortunate we are all in Afghanistan at the moment. You will be contacted in your hotel with our decision.'

'When do you think that might be?'

'It is when it is. Goodbye, Mr Kabu.'

Two of the masked men helped Kabu up from the cushion. They blindfolded him again and led him out to the Land Cruiser.

Many thoughts were going through Kabu's mind on the journey back to his hotel.

Will these terrorists let me go with all that money?

How can I get out of Afghanistan safely? TMA are sure to be monitoring the airport.

Where will the bomb be exploded and how many innocent people will die because of my actions?

The Toyota arrived at the Intercontinental Hotel. Using the delivery entrance, they let Kabu out of the car. They drove off, leaving him to walk around to the main entrance.

Once back in his room he called Ashtak, suggesting they meet for dinner that night. Ashtak recommended a very good Afghani restaurant not far from the hotel.

It was agreed that Kabu would be picked up in front of the hotel at 7 pm.

They asked for a table in the courtyard.

'I met with Abu Bakr al-Baghdadi today.'

'You what? Nobody sees him; he's like a ghost. How in the hell and more importantly, why in the hell?'

'I wasn't going to tell you but I need your help. I have in my possession a one-megaton nuclear device. I have offered to sell it to TMA for $25,000,000.'

'Kabu, you're aware of what TMA is capable of. They will detonate the bomb in a crowded city, killing hundreds of thousands. Can you carry that on your shoulders?'

'Come on Ashtak, even TMA wouldn't detonate a nuclear bomb in a city. I expect they will use it as a great big stick, nothing else. Very similar to what EDO are doing.'

'So that's how you acquired the bomb, you're with EDO.'

'I was, but I'm not anymore.'

'I suppose not, considering you've stolen one of their nuclear bombs.'

'So, are you willing to offer your help?'

'What do you want?'

'I will pay you $100,000 to accompany me to Islamabad. I will pay the Taliban $1,000,000 to escort us both. I also want sufficient protection when I hand over the case; at least six armed guards.'

'That's an awful lot of money, Kabu.'

'It will be worth it.'

'When do you intend to travel?'

'TMA has not agreed to the payment yet. I will have to wait until I hear from them.'

'What if they say no?'

'Then I will have to get in touch with my superiors and confess. Mind you I'll never be able to go back to Fiji again.'

'Let me know when TMA get back to you. My answer is yes I will help you if needed.'

'Thank you, Ashtak.'

December 25

The following morning at breakfast a note in an envelope was delivered to Kabu along with his poached eggs.

You are to be in the car park Bay B at 8am this morning. Look for a Black Range Rover. Get into the back seat. Be sure you are alone.

Kabu checked his watch. It was 7.30 am, just enough time to eat his eggs and drink his coffee.

The Fijian took the lift down to Bay B. He walked along the row of cars looking for the Range Rover and he found it at the end of the car park. With great apprehension, he opened the back door and entered the vehicle. There was one man in the back and two in the front. Nobody spoke. The Range Rover reversed out of the park and exited the car park. Kabu was not required to wear a blindfold this time.

They drove for about fifteen minutes before the driver entered another underground car park. This one was under a four-storey office building. The terrorist in the back seat instructed Kabu to get out and enter the car park office.

Abu Bakr al-Baghdadi was sitting behind an old wooden desk.

'Good morning, Kabu; please take a seat. I apologise for the location but it's secure.'

It certainly is secure what with three men brandishing sub-machineguns just outside the door, Kabu thought.

'I have discussed your offer with the leadership group and we have decided to accept.'

'Excellent.'

'I assume you would like to see the money in your bank account before handing over the goods.'

'Yes, that would be a requirement.'

'Please give me your bank account details.'

'Yes, certainly.'

Swiss National Bank	
IBAN	CH93 0076 2011 6238 5295 7
IBAN Check Digits	93
BBAN	0076 2011 6238 5295 7
Bank Identifier	00762
Account Number	011623852957

'We will deposit the funds today and you should be able to see them tomorrow. That being so, we need to determine the logistics for receiving the goods.'

'I can't call you, I presume, so I suggest you call me tomorrow at say 5 pm,' said Kabu.

'That should give us a week before the device is detonated. That should be enough time.'

'It was a pleasure doing business with you.'

'And you.'

December 26

Kabu received a call from his friend Ashtak confirming that the Taliban had accepted his invitation to escort him safely out of Afghanistan. Payment would be made when Kabu was safely in Islamabad.

He logged into his Swiss National Bank account but the deposit had not yet hit his account. He checked his watch. It was 10 am so maybe a little early. He decided to check again at 11 am.

Kabu tried to watch CNN but couldn't concentrate. He found himself pacing up and down the room. Finally 11 am ticked over. He re-entered the bank web page and logged into his account. He would never be able to describe the feeling of seeing $25,000,000 sitting in his bank account. He could now begin a new life without his beloved Mila.

He called Ashtak and informed him that the money had gone in. He now had to wait for a TMA representative to call to arrange the pickup. He had decided not to include the Griff as part of the deal. He would hold onto the drone for future use.

Kabu went downstairs for lunch. He ordered a Caesar salad and an orange juice, but no wine, as he needed all his faculties.

He returned to his room. He had never experienced an afternoon that went so slowly.

At 4 pm Ashtak called to confirm two vehicles and six armed guards were on standby to escort him to the airport.

At 5 pm his phone rang, and the voice on the other end began to explain to Kabu how he would be picked up in the hotel car park at 6 pm.

'I have made my own arrangements for transport. We will meet you in the car park and you can follow us.'

'That was not my instruction. You need to come with us.'

'I don't think you understand. It's my way or no way.'

'I will have to speak to my superiors. I will call you back.'

Kabu knew he was taking a risk but he also knew it was even riskier being under the control of TMA.

Fifteen minutes later his phone rang.

'OK, we'll follow you.'

'Good, I will see you shortly.'

Kabu phoned Ashtak, informing him they would need to be in the hotel car park at 5.45 pm.

The Fijian captain was used to clandestine operations. He caught the lift down to the car park where he spotted Ashtak standing beside the two Land Cruisers. It would be lucrative being the Toyota dealer in Kabul, he thought.

'Kabu, you get into the front vehicle. You will have three armed guards with you. I will follow, also with three guards. OK, everybody into the vehicles and we'll wait for the nice TMA people.'

They didn't have to wait long. At 6 pm two Land Cruisers entered the car park. Ashtak signalled to them to follow.

The hotel was only sixteen kilometres from Hamid Karzai International Airport and the journey would take only thirty minutes.

Once the convoy arrived at the airport, Kabu and a TMA operative entered the terminal while the others waited in the car park.

Kabu did not communicate with the TMA terrorist. He simply walked to the long-term baggage lockers, unlocked the door and stood back.

The operative extracted the suitcase and without acknowledging Kabu walked back to the car park, slid the case carefully in the back of the Land Cruiser and drove off.

Kabu unlocked the next locker and extracted the box containing the Griff drone. He placed it on a baggage trolley and returned to the car park where Ashtak and his Taliban escort were waiting.

The journey to Islamabad would take eight hours; albeit a very dangerous trip. Ashtak joined his friend in the leading vehicle.

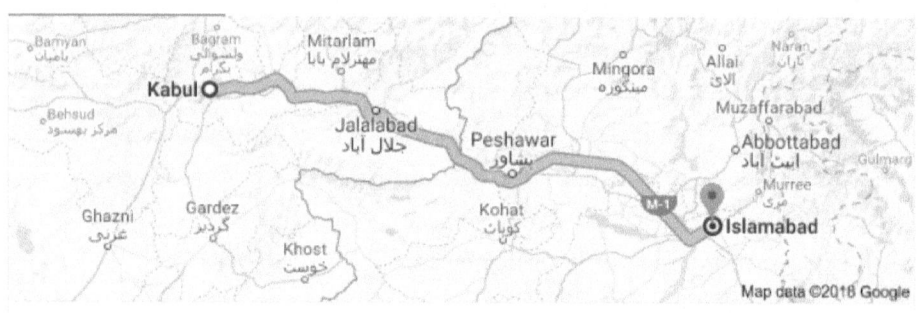

Neither Kabu or Ashtak had visited the infamous Khyber Pass before and it was one part of the trip they were looking forward to.

The Khyber Pass has long been one of the most important trade routes and strategic military locations in the world.

Nestled in the mountains that divide present-day Pakistan and Afghanistan, it forms the bridge between Central and South Asia. Alexander the Great marched his army through the pass in an unsuccessful attempt to capture India in 326 BC. Almost 2,000 years later, Babur did succeed in establishing the Moghul Empire in Northern India after coming through the pass from Afghanistan.

During the Kushan Empire, the pass became a key trade and migration route between India and China. The Silk Road, as it was known, saw the movement of thousands of people, and goods such as wool, cotton, and silk. The Kushan was one of the most multicultural and prosperous empires of its time.

Khyber Pass

The two vehicles drove slowly through the pass, the pace necessitated by the steep and windy road. They were passing through a particularly narrow section when a hail of bullets hit both vehicles. Nobody was hurt as the Land Cruisers were armour plated and the windows and windscreen were also bullet-proof. The drivers speeded up as fast as they dared to go.

Ashtak was concerned that the attackers had rocket launchers. His concerns were vindicated when a rocket hit the rear vehicle. The force of the rocket explosion pushed it over the edge into a steep ravine. The vehicle Ashtak and Kabu were travelling in was able to escape the carnage and they were now in Pakistan; not that that gave them any great comfort.

They had another three hours of driving before they reached the Pakistani capital.

'Who do you think attacked us, Ashtak?'

'Well, we can be certain it wasn't the Taliban. My guess would be TMA.'

'Why TMA? They have the bomb; what more could they want?'

'They probably want their $25,000,000 back.'

'They know it's in a numbered Swiss bank account.'

'Rest assured, Kabu; they would get the number from you.'

'Well, we foiled their attempt.'

'For now. We need to get to Islamabad as soon as possible,' said Ashtak.

'How long will it take us?'

'About three hours as long as we don't encounter any more disruptions.'

'Disruptions? I call it an out-and-out attack,' said Kabu.

'You know what I mean. What are your plans once we arrive in Islamabad?'

'It's only a stopover point. I need to obtain a new passport with a new identity. Before I do that I am going to dye my hair and beard white; not exactly a disguise but it will help.'

'Where to after Islamabad?'

'It's best you don't know, Ashtak, my friend.'

'What can I do to help?'

'Do you know how I can obtain a new passport?'

'Not really, but my comrades may. I'll let you know.'

The two men checked into the Islamabad Serena Hotel, regarded as the city's best.

December 27

At 2 pm Ashtak rang Kabu's doorbell. Ashtak was taken aback. Kabu now had silver hair and beard and he looked very distinguished.

'You look great Kabu; anybody looking for a thirty-eight-year-old Fijian would have trouble identifying you.'

'That's good; how did you go finding a forger?'

'I've located one and we need to be at his studio at 5 pm today.'

'Excellent, how long will it take him?'

'That depends on your nationality.'

'English.'

'In that case, you should have it tomorrow.'

Winter in Siberia

Chapter 23

Suva

December 31

EDO, aka the Prime Minister, Defence Minister and the Minister for the Environment, were staying at the Fijian Resort in Nadi on the pretext of reviewing a white paper on how Fiji was being affected by global warming. In actual fact, they were preparing to view the atomic blast in Siberia.

'Are we fully prepared for the demonstration, Inoke?' asked George.

'I think so, although I haven't heard from Kabu for about a week. I assume everything is under control.'

'He's in a very remote place and it may be that satellite telephones have trouble with reception on the tundra,' said Emori.

'I don't think it will be a problem. He's well trained in what he needs to do,' said Inoke.

Washington December 31

White House Situation Room

The President gathered his war council into the situation room to watch the so-called demonstration.

Present were:

President – Donald Cooper

Vice President – Graham Anderson

Defence Secretary Michelle Bennett

Assistant to the President for National Security Affairs (National Security Advisor) – George Wilson

Secretary of State – William Morris

Director of Central Intelligence Lewis Pentacost

Chairman of the Joint Chiefs of Staff – Hugh Windsor

Attorney General – John Hailes

Secretary of the Treasury – Ian Bryant

Counsellor to the President – Karen Hall

White House Press Secretary – Ari Fletcher

Director of the Federal Bureau of Investigation – Irvine

Deputy Defence Secretary – Paul Wolf

White House Chief of Staff – Andrew Christian

Moscow

January 1

The President of Russia, Alexander Ivanov was presiding over his war cabinet.

Boris Smirnov Directorate KR – External Counter-Intelligence:

Egor Kuznetsov Directorate OT – Operational and Technical Support

Feodore Popov Directorate R – Operational Planning and Analysis:

Gavrie Vasiliev Directorate I – Computer Service

Dusan Sokolov – Directorate of Economic Intelligence

Beijing China

January 1

The Chinese cabinet gathered in the Great Hall of the People.

General Secretary XI Wang

Minister for Foreign Affairs Wang Yo

Minister of National Defence Wei Jinping

Minister for Science and Technology Wang Jie

Minister for Public Security Zhao He

Minister for State Security Guo Quan

Minister for Natural Resources Wang Kezhi

They were all very apprehensive as they knew it would be impossible for China to meet EDO's demands.

New Delhi, India

January 1

The Indian war cabinet gathered in the Prime Minister's office suite to witness the explosion.

Prime Minister Arun Swaraj

Minister for Home Affairs Manohar Jaitley

Minister for Defence Arun Singh

Minister for Coal Harsh Prabhu

Berlin, Germany

December 31

Chancellor Maria Mons

Vice Chancellor Peter Attimair

Economics & Energy Helmut Roth

Defence Julia Kehl

As ten o'clock approached the tension among the world leaders and their cabinet members rose.

Each room was furnished with a 100cm television so they would miss nothing.

Suva Fiji

January 1

Prime Minister Inoke Cakau had the satellite phone in his hand. By sending an encrypted message he would detonate the bomb. He felt at ease knowing the explosion would not harm anyone.

With him were his two co-conspirators.

Finally, the clock on his desk ticked over to 10 am. He sent the message and looked up at the television screen. To his amazement, the tundra remained pristine. He tried sending the message again but still, the vision he received was of snow and nothing else.

'I'm afraid something has gone wrong. Either the device didn't receive the message or there is something wrong with the bomb,' said the Prime Minister.

Tel Aviv 10.15 pm

31 December

Joseph Jacobson and his wife Ruth were enjoying the New Year's Eve celebrations. They were listening to good music with their friends, and they would then move onto a Jaffa restaurant to bring in the New Year.

They left the concert 10.45 pm to walk to the Onza restaurant, one of Jaffa's finest eating-houses.

Joseph had booked a table for 11 pm.

'So, how did everybody enjoy the concert?' asked Joseph.

'I loved it. Four Seasons is one of my favourites,' said Ruth.

The two other couples accompanying them agreed.

'As much as I enjoyed the music, I'm looking forward to supper. I'm famished,' said Maurice.

The group arrived at Onza and were seated at their table. Joseph ordered a bottle of Pelter Pinot Noir, one of Israel's best wines.

Joseph proposed a toast to peace and happiness.

They had no idea TMA had placed the atomic bomb very close to their restaurant.

The restaurant disappeared, as did all the patrons. Onza was very close to ground zero. Jaffa was one of the most popular restaurant districts in Tel Aviv and it was packed with revellers when the explosion occurred.

Tehran Iran

Arash Gilani, his wife Bahar and their two children Mahmoud and Jaleh, lived in an apartment very close to the centre of Tehran. Arash was a software developer and Bahar was a doctor so they were regarded as upper middle-class.

New Year's Eve is not celebrated in Iran although some restaurants cater for it.

Instead, New Year is celebrated at the beginning of spring around the 19th to 21st of March.

The family were all sleeping soundly but unfortunately they never woke up. An Israeli missile carrying a 40-kiloton warhead exploded over the densely populated city at 2 am on New Year's Day in retaliation for the Tel Aviv bomb.

The devastating casualty figures were:
Tel Aviv 200,000
Tehran 1,500,000

The population before the bomb
Tel Aviv 430,000
Tehran 8,500,000

White House Situation Room

'So, I missed a game of golf for this. Obviously, these bastards only had one bomb. I still might be able to get nine holes in.'

The President's red telephone, only used in times of crisis, rang. Everybody in the room had their eyes on the President. He picked up the receiver and listened, and his tanned skin could be seen to turn white.

He returned the receiver to its cradle and looked up at his comrades.

'An atomic bomb exploded over Tel Aviv Israel at 11 pm our time.'

The room erupted into bedlam. "How could this happen?" was the catch cry.

The various cabinet members and the President were discussing their options and trying to determine what rogue nation would commit such an atrocity when the telephone rang again. The President listened. Once again he asked no questions. He just replaced the receiver.

'Ladies and gentlemen, Israel has retaliated by firing a ballistic missile carrying a nuclear warhead into Tehran. We may well be looking at the beginning of World War III.'

Moscow War Room

Alexander Ivanov received the news at fifteen minutes past midnight. He immediately called the entire war council together.

'Do we know who detonated the bomb over Tel Aviv?' asked Ivanov.

'No, but we're sure it wasn't Iran.'

'I can't believe any of Israel's enemies would do this,' said Alexander.

'No, I agree. Every one of them knows Israel has a huge arsenal of atomic weapons so they wouldn't risk it,' said Boris Smirnov.

'Do you think it could be Hamas?' asked Alexander.

'I doubt if they could build a sophisticated nuclear weapon, although Iran could have supplied them with the plutonium,' said Egor.

Well, this is obviously our highest priority. Everybody drop what you were doing. We need to know. I'm about to call the President of the United States and other world leaders. We can't risk this escalating.

Russian War Room

Similar dismay and panic occurred around the world. The overriding question was who started this and how will it end?

138

ARMAGEDDON

CHAPTER 24

Donald Cooper, 47th President of the United States, called his Russian counterpart in Moscow.

Alexander Ivanov took the call in his private office adjoining the war room.

The time in Moscow was 2 am. It was a much more reasonable time of 5 pm in Washington DC.

'Good morning, Alexander.'

'Not such a good morning, Donald. I was just about to call you.'

'You're right; it's a disastrous morning.'

'What's your understanding as to what happened, Donald?'

'All we can ascertain at this early stage is an atomic bomb which we believe was about one megaton in strength exploded in Tel Aviv at 11 pm Israeli time.'

'We don't believe Tehran was responsible. In fact, we don't believe Iran has a nuclear arsenal.'

'Do you think it's an action by a terrorist group?'

'Well, as you know, we were all expecting to see a nuclear explosion in Siberia detonated by EDO. It must seem strange at the very time the Siberian explosion was due to take place a detonation takes place in Israel.'

'Yes, I agree with you, Alexander.'

'We need to ask the Secretary-General to call together the Security Council immediately.'

'I agree,' said the President of the United States.

Suva, January 1

The three members of EDO were dumbstruck. They had just learned of the nuclear blasts in Israel and Iran. They suspected the bomb that exploded in Tel Aviv was the one meant to explode in Siberia.

'How could one of our bombs end up in Israel for God's sake?'

'We find Kabu and we will find out,' said Inoke.

'Rest assured, the major nations of the world will be looking for us,' said George.

'You're right. We need to abandon our campaign for now and stay low,' said Inoke.

'How are we going to live with the blood of millions on our hands?' asked Emori.

'Emori, it's not our fault. As you know, the bombs were not built to create a holocaust; they were built as a big stick a threat to the polluting nations,' said Inoke.

'Remember, it's only us three who know of the plot,' said George.

'I think you may be forgetting Kabu,' said Inoke.

'No, I haven't forgotten him.'

THE TIMES
Digital Archive 1785-2007

To the people of the world; EDO was established to pressure the major polluting countries of the globe to drastically reduce carbon emissions.

The Paris agreement does not go far enough.

We did manufacture six atomic bombs; however, they were not intended to be detonated in anger. Two were to be exploded in very remote locations as a demonstration of our serious intent.

EDO is devastated by the events in the Middle East and apologise that one of its trusted officers provided a bomb to a terrorist organisation which we believe to be TMA.

Although we are still concerned with the pace of global warming we have decided to cease our operations for the time being.

The following newspapers also published the statement.

The Moscow Times

United Nations Security Council

January 2 2023

The five permanent members of the Security Council met in New York:

USA
China
Russia
France
Great Britain

There are ten non-permanent members elected for two-year terms by the General Assembly. At the time of the crisis they were:

Bolivia
Côte d'Ivoire
Equatorial Guinea
Ethiopia
Kazakhstan
Kuwait
Netherlands
Peru
Poland
Sweden

It took a week from the time the Secretary-General called the council together for all the member nations to assemble in New York.

The president for the month of January was Russia.

The Russian Ambassador, Mr Vassily Nebenzia, called the meeting to order.

The permanent members present were:

China. Wu Haitao

France François Delattre

USA Kelley Eckels-Currie

Russia Vassily Nebenzia

Great Britain Karen Pierce

Ambassadors from the non-permanent members were also present.

'Ambassadors, we all know why we are meeting today. We need to address the crisis in the Middle East. Two atomic bombs, both larger than the Hiroshima bomb, exploded over Tel Aviv and Tehran. It is our responsibility to ensure these two horrific events do not develop into a full-scale nuclear war. If it does, it would be the end of mankind as we know it,' said Vassily Nebenzia.

'We, the members of the UN implore that Syria and Iran will take no action against Israel. We also insist Saudi Arabia and Israel refrain from any attack.'

TMA announcement made on YouTube January 8 2023

'The world is asking who detonated the nuclear bomb in Tel Aviv on January 31. It was TMA. Israel is the Muslim world's greatest enemy and deserves to be destroyed. The other great enemy is Iran; the Shiite heretics. We knew the Israelis would assume it was Iran and retaliate. They did our work for us.

There must be no doubt now that TMA has created the next and final Caliphate.

Jerusalem

The Prime Minister and his war cabinet were meeting in the cabinet room in the Knesset. The mood was dire as half the city of Tel Aviv had been destroyed.
Present were:
The Prime Minister Jacob Levy
Defence Minister Alon Biton
Internal Security Minister Ben Auraham
Justice Minister David Kohen
Minister of Finance Dan Cohen

'Do we know the casualty numbers?' asked the Prime Minister.

144

'Our first estimate is 200,000, but we don't know how many will die from radiation poisoning.'

'What's your estimate?'

'Considering it was a ground blast bomb you would expect to double the death rate; however, we are fortunate in that Tel Aviv has a very high number of bomb shelters. Therefore, we are hopeful many residents took advantage. People only need to stay in the shelter for an hour.'

'Well, we can only hope,' said the Prime Minister.

'Sir, may I bring up a major concern?'

'What is it, Alon?'

'It seems Military Headquarters and Mossad's centre of operation were completely destroyed.'

'Are you telling me the complete hierarchy for both the military and Mossad are gone?'

'It would seem so sir,' said Alon.

'When our enemies discover this they could attack while we are down on our knees,' said the Prime Minister.

'There's some more bad news I'm afraid, sir.'

'Go on. You might as well hit me with it.'

'We reacted too quickly. It wasn't Iran who detonated the bomb. It was TMA.'

'Oh good, so we've just destroyed half of Tehran for no reason at all.'

'Apparently, sir.'

'So any empathy we could have expected from the free world has evaporated.'

'Could very well be the case, sir.'

'Let's take a break. I need to call the President of the United States.'

Jacob Levy asked his PA to call the White House and the President agreed to take his call.

'Mr President, thank you for your time.'

'I always have time for you, Jacob. I assume you wish to discuss this terrible business in your part of the world?'

'I do, sir.'

'Please call me Donald. You've known me for long enough.'

145

Jacob told the President everything he knew and apologised for bombing Tehran.

'This is even worse than I first thought. Do you have any senior military personnel remaining?'

'Yes, but we have lost our senior command group.'

'America will continue to support you, Jacob; not with troops but with weaponry.'

'Thank you, Donald. I appreciate it; Israel appreciates it.'

Bodrum, Turkey

Kabu flew from Islamabad to Istanbul, a six and a half hour flight. He connected with a Turkish Airlines flight to Bodrum.

The Bodrum Peninsula is situated on the South West coast of Turkey, surrounded by thirty-two islands and islets, forming a 174km long coastline situated between the bays of Güllük and Gökova. The Peninsula covers an area of 649km² with a population of 120,000.

While in Islamabad, Kabu had searched for an ideal place to live where he wouldn't be recognised. He chose Bodrum in Turkey. The sea and islands reminded him of his homeland of Fiji; a homeland he could never return to.

He spent the first week in a holiday apartment overlooking the harbour. It didn't take him long to discover the home of his dreams. He signed a two-year lease.

It was here in Bodrum that Kabu could spend the rest of his life; or so he thought.

Bodrum Harbour

WAR

WHAT'S IT GOOD FOR?

CHAPTER 25

January 2 2023

The Iranian capital was in complete disarray with people burnt beyond recognition lying dead in the narrow streets and others barely alive, their skin melted from their limbs and faces. Unlike Tel Aviv, Tehran had offered very little protection from the radioactive fallout.

The Israeli missile targeted the lower districts of Tehran Ali Khamenei. The Ayatollah and Hassan Rouhani the President both resided in Upper Tehran. The Israelis didn't want Iran to be in total anarchy as it would be a more dangerous enemy if it were.

Iran had been building military bases in Syria for some time. By the time the missile hit Tehran, Iran had ten large military bases with over 100,000 soldiers located in Syria. An additional 20,000 Iran-trained combatants in Syria were members of Hezbollah, with the rest coming from Lebanon, Iraq, Afghanistan, Pakistan, and other Muslim countries. Iran wasn't about to accept Israel's apology anytime soon.

Tehran

Ali Khamenei, the Ayatollah, and Hassan Rouhani, the President, were meeting in the Ayatollah's modest home.

'We cannot let the Israeli Zionists get away with slaughtering our people,' said Ali Khamenei.

'I agree. If we are going to attack them we need to do it now while they are in turmoil.

January 3 2023, 5am

The Ayatollah ordered Iran to fire 300 long-range missiles at various targets in Israel and Saudi Arabia. At the same time, Iran mobilised 80,000 well-trained troops to cross over the Israeli border.

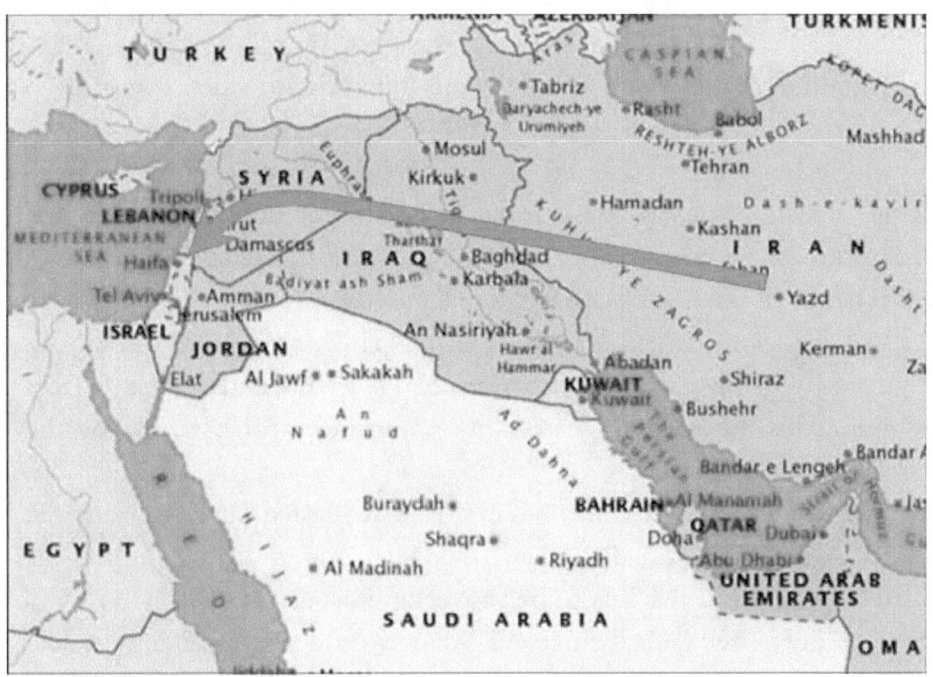

Saudi Arabia responded by sending fifty F35 Strike Fighters on a massive bombing raid, taking out Iran's command headquarters in Syria.

Israel mobilised its regular army and called up its reserves, 600,000 in all. Supporting them were 250 fighter jets including 100 F35 Lightning II's. On the ground there were 2760 tanks, and there was also 10,550 armoured vehicles to reinforce the infantry.

Jerusalem

Jacob Levy and his war cabinet were still in the situation room; sleep was a luxury they could ill afford.

The cabinet had appointed a young colonel, Ben Jacobson, to take charge of the Israeli defence force as the bomb had obliterated the command centre. He was an intelligent, experienced soldier. He was instrumental in Israel's success in the 2006 Lebanon War.

Colonel Jacobson's plan was to create a pincer movement. He moved the majority of his ground troops into Saudi Arabia and then into Iraq. By doing this, he had eliminated any opportunity for a retreat by the Iranian troops.

The Israeli President, Jacob Levy, had requested support from the U.S. 5th Fleet. The U.S. President, Donald Cooper, agreed despite his initial reluctance for the U.S. to be actively involved.

The fleet fired 100 Tomahawk missiles into the attacking Iranian force, which retreated into the arms of the Israeli ground forces. The Iranian forces were defeated inside a week

The Israelis captured a large part of southern Syria, which they would continue to occupy to protect its borders.

Jerusalem January 12

Knesset
Situation room
Present were:
The Prime Minister Jacob Levy
Defence Minister Alon Biton
Internal Security Minister Ben Auraham
Justice Minister David Kohen

Minister of Finance Dan Cohen

Chief of General Staff Colonel Ben Jacobson

Alon Biton spoke for the group.

'Mr Prime Minister, please accept our sympathy for the loss of your son Levy. I knew him personally. He was a fine man and a very good soldier.'

'Thank you, Alon. I appreciate yours and the team's thoughts. I cannot dwell on the loss of Levy. We have a war to win. Colonel Jacobson, would you please bring the war council up to date with our current military situation?'

'Yes, sir. As you are all aware, Iran and Syria launched an attack against Israel in retaliation for Israel detonating an atomic bomb in Tehran.'

'Yes, we are all well aware of that catastrophe, Colonel; a decision I regret, but where do we stand now?'

'With the help of the US 5th Fleet, we were able to contain the enemy forces approximately twenty-five kilometres from Haifa. They are surrounded by Israeli forces on three sides and the 5th Fleet on the Mediterranean Sea.'

'Are we negotiating a surrender?'

'We are hoping they will cooperate.'

'What if they don't?'

'Then I would expect you to give the order to annihilate them.'

'Let's hope it doesn't come to that. What is our casualty rate?'

'Unfortunately, we have 10,000 dead, 15,000 injured or missing.'

'And the enemy?'

'We estimate 30,000 dead 50,000 injured or missing.'

'Have we readjusted the Syrian border to minimise the chances of this happening again?'

'Yes, sir we have moved the border back to Daraa on the Lebanon side and to As Suwayda in the Iranian side. This should give us the buffer we require.'

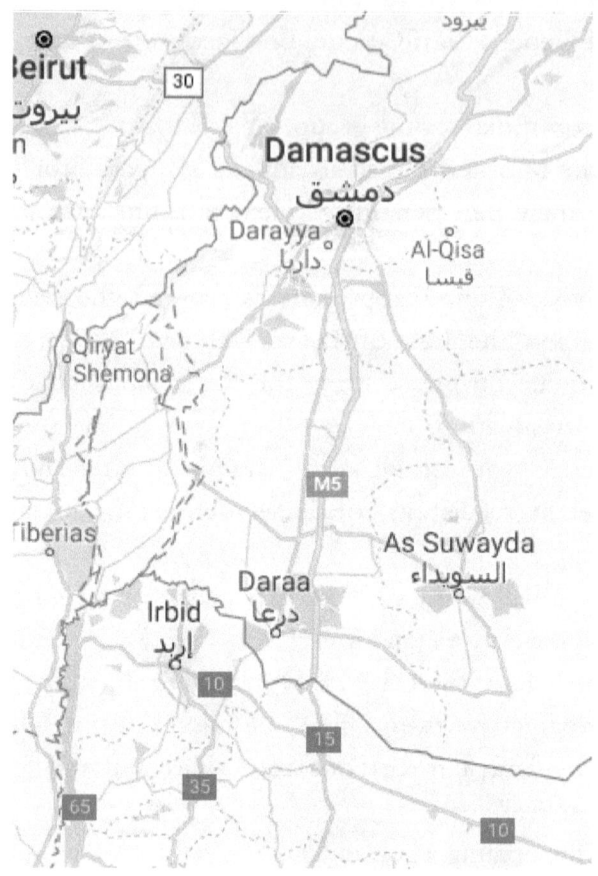

January 15

Iran and Syria agreed to surrender terms with Israel and the Middle East war was over.

Despite providing its allies with weapons, Russia did not get involved in the fighting. World War III was averted.

Moscow

The President of Russia, Alexander Ivanov, made the decision not to get involved in the war. He was angry that the USA had attacked Russia's ally Iran but he was not keen to be involved in an unwinnable war. His decision averted another world war.

There was one thing Russia and the USA agreed on, and that was the destruction of TMA. It was this terrorist group that instigated the war.

They agreed to cooperate and pool their intelligence resources in order to eliminate this evil force.

Washington D.C. - Oval Office

President Cooper was sitting at the resolute desk; the same desk used by Presidents Ronald Regan, Bill Clinton, George W Bush, Barack Obama and Donald Trump.

Resolute Desk

With him were Vice President Graham Anderson and Secretary of State William Morris, plus Secretary of Defence Michelle Bennett.

'It would seem we have averted another world war although the situation in the Middle East is still volatile,' said the President.

'I agree, Mr President. While Israel continues to occupy land in Syria we can't be sure war will not flare up again,' said Michelle Bennett.

'We can't really object to the Israeli occupation as they are only protecting their own borders from invasion,' said William Morris.

'Do we have Israel's word they will never use nuclear weapons again unless attacked themselves?' asked the President.

'Prime Minister Jacobson has given his word.'

'OK I'll approve the acquisition of the new jet fighters, attack helicopters and tanks.'

'I think that's wise, Mr President,' said Graham Anderson.

Suva - January 15

Inoke was eating his breakfast in the Prime Minister's residence. The last few weeks had been extremely stressful. He knew he and his two ministers were ultimately responsible for the death of hundreds of thousands and maybe even millions of innocent people, not to mention being the catalyst for the Middle Eastern war.

His P.A. announced that several visitors wished to see him.

'Strange, I wasn't expecting anyone.'

A tall thickset man in an army uniform strode into the office and addressed the Prime Minister.

'Sir, I'm here to relieve you of your duties.'

'What the fuck?'

'Sir, I must ask you to vacate your office.'

Two large army officers helped the Prime Minister from his chair and escorted him away.

The reason for the coup d'état was that the senior officers in the Fijian military was concerned that the Prime Minister and his inner cabinet seemed preoccupied with other unknown issues and were ignoring the day to day running of the country. The economy was suffering badly.

The officer who led the coup was Colonel Harry Raka, a highly regarded career soldier.

He selected five trusted comrades to work with him until a general election could be called sometime in the future.

Colonel Raka's first task was to review the previous Prime Minister's working papers. He discovered some were missing. He sent a message to Inoke who was now under house arrest but the former PM pleaded ignorance. Colonel Raka suspected the missing papers were contained in the safe located in the PM's office. Only two people knew the combination; the previous Prime Minister and the Attorney General. Colonel Raka knew Inoki would be reluctant to divulge the combination, but the Attorney General was sure to cooperate and he did.

Once Colonel Raka secured access to the safe he began to read the papers. He was horrified by what he read as the entire EDO file including the loss of the Siberian atomic bomb were detailed.

The details of the assassinations of the *Aurarius* crew and the North Korean bomb makers were omitted.

He called a meeting of the junta to discuss the ramifications.

January 17 2023

Colonel Raka and his junta met in the Prime Minister's office.

'Gentlemen I have discovered some very disturbing information about the previous administration. You have all heard of EDO and its mission to reduce global warming. You are also aware that EDO commissioned several atomic bombs to be manufactured on its behalf.

'Well, EDO turns out to be Inoke Cakau, George Finau and Emori Kabu.'

'Are you telling us Fiji has become a terrorist nation?' asked Lieutenant Colonel Temo Ovini.

'So it would seem. I'm sure they thought they were doing the right thing by Fiji, and the planet, however…'

'So what in the fuck do we do now? If we admit EDO was, in fact, three senior ministers of the Fijian Government we will be crucified by the rest of the world,' said Captain Francis Banuve.

'I've thought long and hard about this and my recommendation is we bury it, stay low and do what we do best,' said Colonel Raka.

'And that is?' asked his deputy Colonel George Bokini.

'Continue being a holiday destination.'

'I think you're right.'

'The only issue is…' said Colonel John Atalifo

'What?' asked Colonel Raka

'It would seem we are the proud custodians of four atomic bombs.'

'Yes, what in the hell do we do with them?' asked the Prime Minister.

'Sir, just leave them where they are for the time being.' said George.

'I suppose that's all we can do.'

LOVE AND OTHER BRUISES

CHAPTER 26

Bodrum Turkey

Kabu had only ventured outside his magnificent house once since the bombs were detonated. He was down to eating baked beans for breakfast, lunch, and dinner. He was having trouble sleeping and had taken up smoking again. He had stocked up on cigarettes and whisky but no food items. He spent his days watching Fox's coverage of the Middle East war and the aftermath of the nuclear explosions in Tel Aviv and Tehran. His mood became very dark as he held himself responsible for the death of over one million innocent people.

Once the Middle East war had concluded, Kabu's mood lifted and he ventured into Bodrum and visited the supermarket. He began to eat proper meals although he detested cooking. He hired a cook to come in to prepare his evening meals.

He joined the Bodrum Yacht club and sailed twice a week on Saturdays and Wednesdays. After six months he purchased his own yacht, *Dragonfly.*

Dragonfly

Kabu became an integral member of the yacht club which became his second home. It was here that he met Esma, a beautiful woman who was a psychologist in Istanbul. She visited her ancestral home in Bodrum twice a month. As the relationship between the two flourished, Esma spent more and more time in Bodrum staying at Kabu's magnificent house.

'Darling I never tire from looking at this view. It reminds me of my childhood,' said Esma.

'Yes, I know what you mean, darling. One of the reasons I leased this place was it reminded me of Fiji. It doesn't have the coconut trees or grass huts but the water and the islands offshore are very similar,' said Kabu.

'Do you think we should eat dinner at the yacht club tonight?'

'Would you mind if we stayed in? I don't really feel like going out.'

'No, not at all. I could cook up some köfte if you like.'

'That would be great.'

Esma prepared the köfte patties using ground lamb, served over salads, with yogurt.

Kabu opened a bottle of fine red wine and they ate their dinner on the terrace overlooking the sea.

'Darling, I have some news which you may not like,' said Esma.

'You're leaving me for another man.'

'Don't be silly. You know I would never leave you.'

'So what is this news, Esma?'

'I've been invited to take a study tour of Western Europe's best psychiatric facilities.'

'Congratulations darling; how long will you be away?'

'Three months.'

'My God, three months? How will I survive?'

'Maybe you could meet me in Paris or Berlin for a long weekend.'

'Yes, maybe I could. When do you leave?'

'In four weeks, I know it's short notice but I didn't want to mention it to you until I got confirmation.'

'Well, forget the dishes. Let's go to bed. We only have four weeks.'

'I'm with you, darling.'

The four weeks passed quickly and before they knew it Kabu was kissing the second love of his life goodbye at Istanbul airport.

Esma visited London initially where she spent a week at the Leavey Clinic established by Jo-Ann Leavey.

She spent a second week at the Archways Clinic working with Dr Chris Watson.

The next stop on her agenda was Dublin where she studied psychoanalysis and psychotherapy at Ireland's most respected clinic, Psychotherapy Dublin.

She then flew to Paris. This was the part of the trip she was looking forward to as she would be meeting Kabu after spending four weeks with Estelle Dossin, one of the most respected psychologists in France.

Kabu had booked a suite at the renowned Champs Elysees Plaza Hotel. Esma could hardly wait to see her lover again.

Estelle suggested they eat dinner together on their final night at a small intimate restaurant close to Notre Dame, called Restaurant Paul.

'You have chosen well, Estelle; this is beautiful.'

'I think you will enjoy the menu also. Paul is a two hat Michelin chef.'

'Would you mind if I chose the wine?' asked Esma.

'Please go ahead.'

'Would you prefer white or red?'

'I would prefer red if that's OK.'

Esma examined the wine list. She decided on a Mouton-Cadet Bordeaux, not the most expensive wine on the list but nevertheless highly rated.

The waiter offered the wine to Esma to taste.

'Thank you, it's excellent.'

He then poured a glass for Estelle and then Esma.

'So, to new and lasting friendships,' said Estelle.

'To new and lasting friendships,' said Esma raising her glass.

As they were discussing their month together a man in a black hoodie brandishing an AK47 began shooting at all the restaurant patrons.

The lone wolf walked slowly through Paul's killing people methodically, and each time he made a hit he yelled, *Allahu Akbar.*

Esma and Estelle had hidden under their table when they heard the first shots. They didn't say a word to each other but their terrified eyes communicated all.

The shooting ceased and the two terrified woman hoped that was the end of it. To be sure, they stayed under the table.

Esma felt a presence behind her. She turned around, only to see the terrorist.

He smiled and whispered, "*Allahu Akbar*," and put three bullets into her head. Estelle was next.

The terrorist managed to kill sixteen innocent people.

He yelled *Allahu Akbar* the entire time he was shooting. A gendarme heard the shooting and ran to the restaurant where he fired on the terrorist, killing him instantly.

Kabu had landed at Charles de Gaulle Airport around about the time of the terrorist attack. He watched the CNN report when he arrived at the hotel. He started to become concerned when Esma had not arrived at the hotel by midnight. At 1.00 am he decided to contact the police. The closest station was Commissariat de Police 1 Avenue du General Eisenhower.

He approached the officer on the front desk.

'Excuse me, officer, I'm afraid I speak very little French. My partner has not arrived at my hotel. I'm concerned she may have been involved in the restaurant shooting.'

'What is her name?'

'Esma Arsian. She's Turkish.'

'Let me see if she's been identified.' The policeman entered the system and began to interrogate the database looking for Esma's name. It didn't take him long before he looked up at Kabu and confirmed Esma had been shot and died at the scene.

Kabu was numb; he just stood at the counter not knowing what to do.

Finally, the policeman asked Kabu if there was anything he could do to help.

'No.'

'Can I get your details? I'm afraid we will need to get in contact with you to identify the body.'

'If you must.'

Kabu had identified a woman he loved before and he did not look forward to doing it again.

When Kabu returned to the hotel, he pulled out the small black box from his luggage and opened it. The grieving lover just stared at the three-carat diamond ring he had purchased at Tiffany & Co. He had planned to ask Esma to marry him the next day.

Kabu boarded a plane for Bodrum the next day. Esma's casket was in the hold. He then flew to Istanbul to attend Esma's funeral; being a Muslim she needed to be buried as soon as possible.

There were two hundred mourners in the Blue Mosque, as Esma and her family were very highly regarded in Istanbul.

Blue Mosque

Kabu flew back to Bodrum the day after Esma's funeral and the next morning he visited the yacht club. The few members that were there that morning were surprised to see him so soon after the funeral.

Kabu greeted them as though there was nothing wrong. He untied *Dragonfly* and motored out of the harbour and that was the last time anybody saw Kabu. Despite an extensive search neither he nor *Dragonfly* was found.

He donated $8,000,000 to the survivors of the two bombs to be distributed by the Red Cross.

THE RUSSIAN MAFIA

CHAPTER 27

The four men were eating in a stylish Moscow restaurant, Café Pushkin. All wore expensive suits complemented by expensive silk ties and handkerchiefs in their top suit pockets. They could be bankers or businessmen or even recruitment consultants.

Cafe Pushkin Moscow

The fact was all of these men were active members of the Vory, the most powerful crime group in Russia with very strong international connections.

They laundered more money than any other group in the country (Bankers).

They managed not only criminal activities but also legitimate companies. (Businessmen)

They controlled the people smuggling market in Europe. (Recruitment Specialists)

The senior person of the group, Dmitri Belkin, brought up the topic of the missing nuclear devices.

'Has everybody heard of these four one-megaton bombs that have gone missing?'

'You mean the bombs that the terrorist group who call themselves EDO say they have?' said Dannill Agin.

'Oh, they have them all right. They detonated one near Fiji and it was one of their bombs that blew up half of Tel Aviv,' said Dmitri.

'I thought it is was TMA who blew up Tel Aviv,' said Alexey Davidoff.

'TMA wouldn't know how to make a bed let alone make an atomic bomb. My bet is they purchased it off EDO or one of their people that had turned.

'My point is there are four sophisticated atomic bombs located in New York, Berlin, Beijing, and New Delhi. There was one in Moscow but I believe that's the one they sold to TMA. I suggest we find them, steal them, and sell them to the highest bidder,' said Dimitri.

'How much do you think we could get for each bomb, Dmitri?'

'Hard to know, Alexey. I would suggest somewhere around $20,000,000.'

'My God; you think that much?'

'Yes, I do— these aren't items you can buy in a supermarket.'

'The CIA, MI5 and various other agencies have been looking for these bombs for some time. What makes you think we can find them, Dmitri?'

'We don't have the same restrictions as government agencies. We can torture or kill who we want when we want.'

'That's a good point.'

'Right, this is our number one priority, comrades; let's find these bombs.'

The four men returned to their respective divisions. Each had a speciality.

Dmitri controlled the manpower, the gangsters that performed the dirty work.

Dannill was in charge of Information Technology and his group could hack into any computer network in the world.

Alexey's responsibility was armoury; whether it was an AK47 or a guided missile he could procure it. His group also maintained the weapons.

Sergey's division encompassed drug distribution and finance.

The first part of the trail led Dmitri and four operatives to New York. They suspected the hit on Richard Manson was more than a competitive business exercise as was widely believed.

They contacted their New York Mafia colleagues to ascertain if anything was known in relation to who ordered the hit.

The Mafia was aware of who carried out the job but were unaware who actually ordered it. Dmitri was given the hit man's contact details and a visit was planned for the next day.

Dmitri and two of his men drove to an address in Queens 34/21st Avenue.

They knocked on the front door and a slim Chinese gentleman opened it.

'Hello, we are hoping to contact Henry Yunnan. Is that you?'

'That depends on who's asking. Who the fuck are you and what do you want?'

'Please forgive me. My name is Dmitri Belkin. I'm a senior member of the Vory.'

Dmitri and his two accomplices pulled out their Glock pistols, both with silencers, and pointed them at the very nervous Chinese man.

'We'd like to come inside for a chat if you don't mind.'

Henry reluctantly agreed to show Dmitri and his men into the front parlour.

'So, how can I help you?'

'We understand you conducted a hit on a fellow called Richard Manson in September 2020.'

'I don't know what you're talking about.'

'Henry, we don't care how many hits you've done. God knows we've done plenty.'

'I'm serious. I have no idea what you're talking about. I've never heard of Richard Manson let alone topped him.'

'Really? Well let's see if we can jog your memory,' said Dmitri.

The Vory boss nodded at Dannill who pointed his Glock at the Chinese man's left knee and pulled the trigger.

Henry screamed, holding his shattered left kneecap.

'OK, Henry. Who ordered the hit?'

'I honestly don't know. I received the instruction anonymously. He insisted on not divulging his identity.'

'How were you paid?'

'A bank draft from ANZ Suva Fiji.'

'Why Suva?'

'I don't know.'

'OK, Henry, we'll leave you alone, but if we find you've been lying to us we'll be very unhappy and so will you.'

The three men left young Henry to get himself to the hospital for some much-needed medical treatment.

'So where from here?' asked Davydov.

'It's interesting that the draft was drawn on a Fijian bank, albeit an Australian-based bank,' said Dmitri.

'Wasn't Manson's salvage ship searching in Fijian waters?' asked Ivanov.

'Yes, so I understand. It was common knowledge he was hoping to discover the wreck of the *Vanderbilt* and its gold shipment.'

'Don't you think it is a coincidence that Manson was hit and his ship disappeared without a trace all about the same time?' asked Ivanov.

'It does seem a little coincidental, doesn't it? I think we need to fly to Suva. Have you ever been there?'

'No, I've never visited the Southern Hemisphere.'

Dmitri booked three business class fares using his black American Express credit card.

They booked into the Grand Pacific Hotel, regarded as Suva's finest.

After breakfast, Dmitri arranged a car and driver to take them to the construction site of the nuclear reactor. He was keen to discover why the nuclear scientists were returning home without having finished their contract. The fact that they were all killed in a plane crash made it even more mysterious.

The car pulled up outside the construction site fence.

There was no doubt it was a major construction site, yet there was no activity whatsoever. Based on the amount of rust on some of the equipment, it was obvious no work had taken place for some time.

'There's no way they produced plutonium from here. It's not even close to being operational,' said Dannill.

'I think we've been barking up the wrong tree. I can't see how Fiji could be involved in EDO or producing atomic bombs,' said Davidov.

'Let's not jump to conclusions just yet. There are other options to explore,' said Dmitri.

THE ART OF PERSUASION

CHAPTER 28

Paying for information was of no consequence to Dmitri; Vory had vast resources at its disposal.

He decided he needed to establish who was on Patrol Boat 203, which was used to search for the *Aurarius*. They needed to discover a crewman, who could help them in their search.

He obtained the crew list from a friendly and now wealthy petty officer.

Dmitri decided to approach a sailor rather than the captain as he felt a lowly paid sailor would be more easily influenced than an officer.

Dmitri chose Joseph Banuve, a lowly seaman who was known to drink at the Cutty Sark Bar and Grill.

Dmitri and his two comrades, Dannill and Davidov, entered the Cutty Sark and asked the barman if Joseph was present.

'Yeah, that's him sitting over there.'

The Russian gangsters walked over, introducing themselves as Russian businessmen who were looking to establish a luxury cruise service in Fiji.

'Joseph, you have been recommended to us as being a very capable seaman. We also understand you will be discharged from the Navy in two months. Would you be interested in joining our crew? We will pay you well.'

'How much are you paying?'

'This isn't the place to discuss such matters, so why don't we meet at our hotel tomorrow?' said Dmitri.

'OK, what hotel and what time?'

'Grand Pacific Hotel at 10 am.'

'I'll be there.'

'He seems to be a man of few words, Dmitri. Are you sure we will obtain the information we need?' asked Dannill.

'Don't worry, we will get what we need one way or another,' said Dmitri.

Joseph arrived on time and asked reception to contact Dmitri, who gave permission for the young sailor to come up to his suite.

Joseph rang the bell and Davidov answered the door, showing him in.

'Can I get you a drink, Joseph?'

'No, thank you.'

'OK, let's get down to business. I believe you were a crewmember on Patrol Boat 203 searching for the *Aurarius*. Is that correct?'

'Hold on. I thought I was here to discuss my possible future employment?'

'Actually, no— that was a ploy to get you here,' said Dmitri. 'Let me explain the rules to you. If you tell us exactly what happened to the *Aurarius* and her crew, we will let you go with $5000 in your pocket. If you fuck us about we will shatter both your kneecaps; simple rules really.'

Joseph knew they weren't joking and he decided the easier option was to tell all and walk away with the money.

The young sailor described how the Special Forces boarded the ship and eliminated all on board. He also described how the ship was blown up and sunk without a trace.

'Why did the navy do such a thing?'

'It had something to do with two objects salvaged from the ocean floor. It was all hush-hush.'

'Thank you, Joseph; you've done well. Give me your bank details and the money will be deposited tomorrow.'

Once the sailor had departed, the three Russians discussed what they had discovered.

'I think the key must be what was salvaged by the *Aurarius*. What could be worth killing the entire ship's crew for? It wouldn't be treasure. The booty would be shared by the salvage company and the Fijian Government.'

167

'We need to do some more investigating. In the meantime, let's go over what we know.

'Six nuclear scientists are recruited from North Korea to design and build a nuclear reactor.

'All six died in a plane crash along with the pilot.

'The reactor is nowhere finished.

'The *Aurarius* disappears below the sea, taking all crew with it. We now know how but not why.

'Richard Manson is killed in a hit and run in New York. We know it was a professional hit. We don't know who commissioned it, but we have our suspicions.

'In the space of three years, there are two coups in Fiji.'

'What is the name of the previous Prime Minister?' asked Dmitri.

'Inoke Cakau,' answered Dannill.

'Is he being held in prison?'

'No, he's under house arrest.'

'I want you to find out the address of the house and how many guards there are. I'd like to have a chat with him.'

'Yes, Dmitri.'

Davidov reported back to Dmitri, having discovered Inoke Cakau's location.

'I now know where the former Prime Minister resides. He's not far out of Nadi in a magnificent beachside mansion.'

'Excellent, that means we can come in from the sea, take him and interrogate him elsewhere. Davidov, I want you to rent a house reasonably close and procure a fast speedboat.'

Davidov rented a modest four-bedroom bungalow ten kilometres from the ex-Prime Minister's mansion. He was also able to hire a suitable speedboat.

RUSSIAN ROULETTE

CHAPTER 29

'Do we know how many guards there are?'

'Just two — both SAS.'

'Well, they're not just going to lay their guns down and behave, are they? They'll be carrying automatic weapons and we need to do the same.'

The weapons they would use would be AKS-74U; the rifle the elite Russian military deploys.

Dmitri waited for a dark night as the last thing he wanted was a full moon. He had to wait five days for a crescent moon with an abundance of dark clouds covering the night sky.

The three Russian gangsters boarded the boat and headed off at speed for the Ex-PM's mansion; a trip that took them five minutes. As they approached, Dmitri slowed down to five knots and coasted to the landing.

The three men had their faces blackened and were wearing black clothing.

They moved slowly along the landing, keeping low the whole way. When they reached the end, they could see into what they thought was the living room. A very large television was mounted on the wall and Inoke was watching a game of rugby between Fiji and Australia. Sitting behind him was a soldier holding an AK47 assault rifle. The Fijian Government had recently received a donation of $10,000,000 worth of weapons, including a shipment of AK 47s from Russia of all places.

Dmitri was concerned that they could see only one soldier; where was the other one? His trepidation faded when he sighted the second soldier enter the room with three cans of beer.

Drinking on duty. I don't think their superior officer would like that, thought Dmitri.

He nodded to the other two men and on a silent count of three they opened the sliding door and shot the two soldiers before they could register what was going on.

Inoke was in total shock. His immediate reaction was to shout, 'Don't shoot me.'

'Don't worry, we have no intention of shooting you... we just want you to come with us.'

'Why, where are you taking me?'

'Not far. We just want a chat about a few things like atomic bombs.'

'I have no idea what you're talking about.'

'If you are having trouble recalling, we have methods which will help you remember. Now come on, we have a boat at the end of the jetty and we need to get moving.'

Davidov and Dannill escorted the petrified Fijian, now in handcuffs, to the boat. Once everybody was aboard they took off at speed, arriving at the bungalow in a few minutes. Inoke had been blindfolded for the trip and remained so until he entered a bedroom.

'What happens now?' said Inoke.

'You stay locked in this room until we decide to question you,' said Davidov.

'It doesn't have a TV. I'll miss the game.'

'I think that will be the least of your worries. If I were you, I'd be thinking about atomic bombs.'

'I've told you I know nothing about atomic bombs.'

'We'll see.'

Inoke was imprisoned for the remainder of the night.

Dannill brought him his breakfast first thing in the morning. It consisted of cereal, cold toast and jam. He returned with a mug of tea.

After breakfast, he was allowed to shower and the Russians provided him with a black tracksuit and some underwear.

Later that morning, the three Russians entered the room. Davidov was carrying a gas mask.

'Sit on this chair, Inoke, with your hands behind your back.'

'What if I refuse?'

Dannill hit the Fijian in the stomach, winding him.

'Now I'll ask you once again to sit down with your hands behind you,' said Dmitri.

This time the Fijian complied and Davidov handcuffed him. The gas mask was placed over Inoke's head.

'This how this game works. We call this the elephant. When you've had enough and wish to answer my questions you will nod your head. Is that clear?'

The Russians gave the ex-PM time to get used to breathing in the mask. Then Davidov hit him hard in the stomach while Dannill squeezed the tube, cutting off Inoke's air. The Russians watched as the Fijian gasped for air. After one minute, they released the pressure on the hose, allowing air to enter the mask again. They repeated this procedure twice more until Inoke nodded that he'd had enough.

Davidov undid the handcuffs and gave Inoke a glass of water. They left him in the room alone for fifteen minutes to recuperate.

When Dmitri and his two comrades returned, Inoke looked quite petrified.

'Shall we begin with the salvage operation? Did the *Aurarius* recover two atomic bombs from the sea floor?'

'I believe so.'

'That's not good enough, Inoke. I want a yes or no answer.'

'Yes, they came from an American fighter plane that had fallen off an aircraft carrier.'

'Where were the bombs moved to?'

'A warehouse on the navy base.'

'You're doing very well, Inoke.'

'Did you hire the North Korean nuclear scientists to make the six bombs using the material from the salvaged bombs?'

'Yes.'

'Were they successful?'

'Yes.'

'What happened to the North Koreans once they had completed their assignment.'

'We eliminated them.'

'Just like you eliminated the crew of the *Aurarius*?'

'Yes.'

'Did you organise the hit on Richard Manson?'

'Yes.'

'You detonated one of the bombs in the Pacific, did you not?'

'We did.'

'Who's we?'

'My two colleagues in EDO.'

'Who are they?'

'I'd rather not say; they can't help you.'

'Would you like the gas mask again, Inoke?'

'George Finau and Emori Apolosi.'

'Who are they?'

'George was my Defence Minister and Emori was Minister for the Environment.'

'How did TMA get possession of the bomb which was detonated in Tel Aviv?

'I'm not sure, but we believe the Fijian army captain we assigned to manage the Siberian blast turned traitor.'

'What's his name?'

'Captain Kabu Vula.'

'Do you know where he is now?'

'No.'

'Now for the big question, Inoke; where are the remaining bombs located?'

'They are in the storeroom of the Fijian embassies in Berlin, Beijing, New Delhi and the consulate in New York.'

'Thank you Inoke, you've done very well,' said Dmitri.

The senior Vory boss nodded to his comrades. As he left the room, both opened fire with their AKS-74U's, leaving the bloodied corpse of the ex-Prime Minister on the bedroom floor.

The cleaner can clean that up, Dmitri thought.

EVERY PICTURE TELLS A VORY

CHAPTER 30

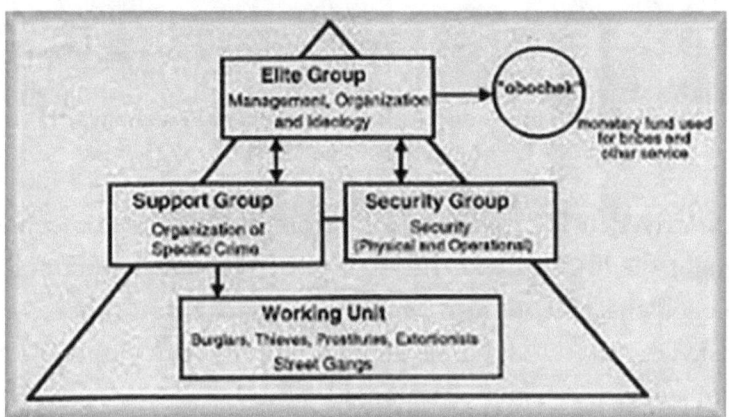

Vory Hierarchy Chart

Dmitri and his working unit made their way to Nadi International Airport where Dmitri purchased three business class tickets to Moscow, flying Emirates via Dubai.

After an uneventful flight incorporating a day and a half of sitting on a plane, they arrived in Moscow.

Dmitri spent the first day back resting, hoping jet lag would not dim his mind for his meeting with Grigory Popov, Vory's head of the Elite Group.

The Russian Mafia, Vory, operated like any other corporation with a hierarchy and operational divisions. They even had their head office located in the middle of the CBD of Moscow.

**Vory's head office address Presnenskaya naberezhnaya,
12, Moskva, Russia, 123317**

Dmitri arrived at HQ ten minutes before his scheduled meeting time and he caught the lift to the twenty-first floor. The lift doors opened and he approached the receptionist. She was similar to any other corporate receptionist; very pretty and well dressed. She invited Dmitri to sit and offered him a coffee, which he accepted.

After a twenty minute wait Grigory Popov asked his receptionist to show Dmitri into his large palatial office overlooking Red Square.

'Good morning, Dmitri; it is good to see you. Please take a seat. Would you like a coffee or a tea?'

'No thank you, Grigory, I just had a coffee.'

'So, how's your family?'

'They're all good, thank you. The youngest boy Anatoly has been selected for the under 19 national soccer team.'

'That's excellent and what of the older boy?'

'Luka is in his third year at university studying medicine.'

'And how's your new wife? I believe she is quite a bit younger than you?'

'She's very well and we now have a little girl— Tanya.'

'You must be very proud, Dmitri.'

'Yes, Grigory. I must admit I am.'

'Right, let's talk business. Please brief me.'

Dmitri briefed the head of Vory with the details of his trip from New York to Fiji.

'So, Dmitri, we now know there are four one-megaton atomic bombs located in four cities.'

'That's correct. Not only that, but we now know where they are being stored.'

'Do we? Where?'

'In the storeroom of the Fijian embassy in each city.'

'What is your proposed plan?'

'I suggest we break into the embassy storerooms, take the bombs which are apparently quite light, and move them to a safe location.'

'Are you proposing we sell them to a rogue nation like Iran?'

'No, what I suggest is they become a major source of income for Vory.'

'How so?'

'We target the G7 nations and threaten to detonate a bomb in their capital cities unless they pay Vory a fee of $20,000,000 a year.'

'That's a lot of money, Dmitri; are you sure they would pay up?'

'With respect, Grigory, that's about how much these countries spend on travel and entertainment in a year.'

'So you believe we could generate $20,000,000 annually?'

'No sir, $140,000,000 a year.'

'My God. How do you propose we retrieve the bombs from the embassies?'

'I don't know yet but I would require support from the organisation to devise and execute the plan.'

'You have my full support and any resources you need.'

'Thank you, Grigory.'

'It was good to see you again. Good luck with the plan and keep me informed.'

'Thank you. I will.'

Diplomacy

Dmitri discussed the situation with a number of senior operatives and it became apparent there were two alternatives.

- Break into the Fijian embassies and take the bombs by force, killing whoever gets in the way.
- Bribe an embassy official to hand over the suitcase containing the bomb, replacing it with a replica to avert suspicion.

'I think if we stormed the embassy the world would wonder why an inconsequential archipelago in the Pacific received such attention,' said Alexey Gorky.

'I agree, Alexey. The amount we would have to pay would be minimal compared to the return on investment,' said Dmitri.

'How much should we offer the embassy staff?' asked Sergey.

'I'd expect about $100,000,' said Dmitri.

'You will no doubt have to get approval from Grigory.'

'Yes, I'll arrange to see him as soon as possible.'

THE NOT SO UNITED NATIONS

CHAPTER 31

The United Nations Security Council was meeting for the first time since the war in the Middle East. They had a lot to discuss such as the rebuilding of Tel Aviv and Tehran as well as Israel's occupation of southern Syria. All were on the council's agenda.

The other major issue was EDO and the countries targeted to dramatically reduce their greenhouse emissions.

The chair for the meeting was the United States. Kelly Eckels-Currie was the UN ambassador.

'Good morning ladies and gentlemen; we have a full agenda so let me get started with Tel Aviv and Tehran.

'As you are all aware, both cities suffered horrendous casualties as well as damage to the cities themselves. May I suggest a vote for the members of the UN Security Council to donate money and resources to help these two countries rebuild. With luck, other countries will follow our lead.'

Although the motion was carried no member specified the amount they were willing to donate.

The next point of discussion was Syria.

Russia and China proposed a motion insisting Israel withdraw back to its original borders.

The USA vetoed the motion.

It was now time to discuss EDO and global warming. All the nations present had made significant inroads into reducing their carbon footprint. A significant number of coal-fired power stations had been retired.

A policy of encouraging electric cars had also been implemented.

Despite not hearing from EDO for some time, they all knew it was only a matter of time. Any organisation that had an arsenal of nuclear weapons must be feared.

Moscow

Grigory Popov was reading Pravda while waiting for his trusted Lieutenant Dmitri Belkin to arrive to update him on the nuclear bomb scheme.

His secretary informed him that Dmitri had arrived and was waiting to be shown into his office.

'Show him in, Sasha.'

'Hello, Dmitri, take a seat; would you care for coffee or tea?'

'Yes, Grigory I would like a tea, please.'

The Chairman of Vory used the intercom to order a tea for his guest and a coffee for himself.

Once settled, Grigory asked the inevitable question.

'Dmitri, what is the plan to secure these bombs?'

The senior Vory operative briefed his boss in full and Grigory approved the bribes to secure the suitcases being held in the Fijian embassies.

Dmitri left Grigory's office satisfied that he would soon be heading up the most successful and lucrative project in the organisation's history.

He put a small team together, comprised of Dannill Agin, Alexey Petrov, and Sergey Galkin.

Their first destination was New York.

The address of the consulate was East 45th Street. Dmitri booked four rooms in the famous Algonquin Hotel on 44th Street.

Algonquin Hotel

Dannill was given the task of discovering how many staff was based in the consulate and who would be the most vulnerable. Time was of the essence; therefore he was permitted to hire a private detective to choose a likely candidate who was likely accept a bribe.

There was only three diplomatic staff attached to the consulate; the First Secretary, the Second Secretary and the chauffeur. It was the Second Secretary who was chosen to work with the Russians. They chose Jesoni Kepa due to his weakness for gambling.

Dannill and Alexey approached Jesoni as he was leaving the Consulate to go home.

'Hi, Jesoni, my name is Dannill and this is Alexey; can we have a word with you?'

'Why? I don't know you do I?'

'No, you don't know us but we could be your best friends.'

'What do you mean?'

'Just come with us where we can talk in private and we can tell you how to make an easy $100,000.'

'How do I know I can trust you?'

'Here's a down payment.'

Dannill handed Jesoni $10,000 in a brown paper envelope.

'OK, you've convinced me. I'll go with you. Where are we going?'

'To our hotel, the Algonquin; it's in the next street.'

'I know where it is.'

The three men walked to the hotel and caught the quaint lift up to the sixth floor.

Dannill opened room 605 with his key card Alexey and Jesoni followed him in. Dmitri joined them.

'OK, Jesoni this is what you need to do. We want you to go into the Consulate's storeroom where you will find a suitcase. We want you to photograph it from all sides and send the photos to my phone. My number is 6238 3444,' said Dmitri.

'Is that all you want me to do?'

'No, that's stage one. We will tell you what stage two is once you have completed the first stage.'

'Can I go now?'

'Yes, Jesoni you can go now. I look forward to receiving the photos.'

Jesoni had entered the storeroom many times to retrieve stationary and other office items but he had never noticed a suitcase.

He stayed back working the following night. When the other two had left the building he made his way to the storeroom. He didn't find the suitcase in his initial sweep but he noticed a tarpaulin covering some sort of object. He pulled it back and to his delight found the suitcase with diplomatic stickers covering it. He used his phone to take the photos and sent them to Dmitri.

Dmitri was delighted as he showed his comrades the photos. 'This is a standard Samsonite suitcase albeit red. We will be able to purchase a duplicate from any luggage store.'

Dmitri directed Alexey to The Big Bag near Broadway where he purchased the suitcase and brought it back to Dmitri's room.

'Excellent, Alexey. Now I want to go to the Strand bookstore and purchase some books.'

'Forgive me for questioning you Dmitri, but why?'

'We need something that has the same weight as the bomb. I want you to purchase books on Global Warming.'

The books purchased were:

'We need diplomatic tape. Where can we get a roll of that?' asked Dannill.

'That's up to Jesoni.'

Dmitri contacted Jesoni, instructing him to collect the suitcase.

'Jesoni, take this suitcase and swap it with the one in the storeroom. Wrap diplomatic tape around it just like the original. Bring it back here and collect the $90,000 balance.'

Jesoni did as he was instructed, returning with the suitcase. Dmitri transferred the money into the Fijian's bank account.

Dmitri sent a code to Grigory in Moscow indicating the first bomb had been retrieved.

Head Office had arranged for a forged diplomatic passport for Dmitri and he would bring the suitcase back to Moscow.

He passed through passport control and customs without a hitch and was soon flying back to Russia.

The suitcase didn't need to pass through customs. Dmitri signed for it and the one-megaton bomb was placed in the boot of the BMW which was sent to meet him.

Dmitri went straight to his superior's office despite his jet lag.

Grigory welcomed him. 'So, I'm delighted the mission was successful Dmitri.'

'Yes, sir; one down and three to go.'

'I will pass the suitcase over to one of our top technical teams as we don't want to detonate it prematurely.'

'Please let me know how it goes, sir.'

'I will now you go home and get some sleep.'

'Thank you, Grigory, I will.'

Dmitri caught a taxi to his newly acquired apartment in a renovated factory building called the Bolshevik.

His family was there to greet him and he then went to bed, sleeping for eight hours.

His wife Nikita woke him.

'I'm sorry to disturb you, darling, but Grigory is demanding to speak with you.'

'OK, can you tell him I'll be with him in a minute?'

Dmitri washed his face and combed his hair. He now felt half decent.

'Hello, Grigory, how can I help you?'

'We were able to open the suitcase without incident.'

'That's good. How does it look?'

'It looks like a whole lot of New Yorker magazines.'

'What do you mean?'

'Exactly what I said. There is no fucking bomb, just fucking magazines.'

'That Fijian bastard must have done a swap.'

'What bastard?'

'The Fijian from the Fijian Consulate.'

'Well, I suggest you and the two operatives you had with you get back to New York quick smart and have a chat with him.'

'Yes, sir.'

NEEDLE IN A HAYSTACK

CHAPTER 32

Dmitri, Dannill, and Alexey flew back to New York to try and discover what happened to the bomb. The first stop was the Fijian Consulate.

Dmitri entered the building located at East 45th Street and caught the lift to the 10th floor. He approached the counter where a black American woman asked if she could help.

'Yes, I would like to speak to Jesoni Kepa if I could please.'

'I'm sorry, but he is no longer with us. He has returned to Fiji.'

'Did he leave an address in Fiji?'

'He did say he was returning to his village. Wherever that is I'm not sure.'

'I asked Jesoni to hold onto my suitcase until I returned to New York. He agreed and placed it in the storeroom. Could I have it back please?'

'I go into the storeroom regularly. I don't recall seeing a suitcase. You're more than welcome to look for yourself.'

'Thank you.'

Dmitri entered the storeroom accompanied by the woman. He looked everywhere but could not find the red suitcase. He thanked her and left the consulate and checked into the Algonquin.

He called the other two Russians to his room to determine their next step.

'The suitcase is definitely not in the consulate's storeroom. The bastard has either taken it back to Fiji with him or somebody else has got involved.'

'Should we go to Fiji and track him down?' said Dannill.

'The problem with that idea is he's gone back to his village making it almost impossible to find him. The villagers are a tight-knit group and they would never divulge his whereabouts,' said Dmitri. 'I'm going to recommend to Grigory that we retrieve a suitcase from another Fijian embassy.'

'Which embassy?'

'It doesn't really matter, Alexey, although I would lean to Germany.'

Dmitri called Grigory, and updated him on the lost bomb in New York. 'I think we need to establish if this was a one-off and the other bombs are still in place.'

'Yes, I think you're right. Go to Berlin and bring me back a bomb, not old magazines.'

'Yes, sir.'

The three Vory operatives flew to Berlin and checked into the Sofitel.

Dmitri hired a private detective to select an embassy employee who would be susceptible to bribe. He recommended Vijay Bari, First Secretary of the embassy. The reason he was chosen was he was a father of three and had a pregnant wife. He was also conducting an affair with his German PA Nadine Wagner; therefore he was vulnerable.

Dannill and Alexey approached Vijay as he was leaving the embassy to meet Nadine.

'Excuse me, Vijay, my name is Alexey and this is my colleague Dannill. I was wondering if we could have a chat?'

'Why?'

'You don't know us but we know you.'

'How so?'

'We know you have a wife and three children with another one on the way. We also know you're fucking your PA on the side.'

'What's this about? Are you trying to blackmail me?'

'We just want to talk to you about a business proposition.'

'OK, there is a café around the corner that's very private.'

Once the three men settled into the booth at the rear of the café Dannill opened the conversation. He explained about the red suitcase and how it needed to be swapped. The fee was also mentioned as $100,000, which certainly lifted Vijay's interest.

The Fijian diplomat agreed to take part in the swap. He asked no questions as to the contents of the suitcase.

The method remained the same; first photos, then purchase suitcase, fill it with books and lead, tape and place it in the storeroom and bring the original back to the hotel.

The Russians waited anxiously for Vijay to return to the Sofitel and they didn't have to wait long. Once it was delivered, Dmitri transferred the money to the Fijian's bank account.

Next day, the three gangsters flew back to Moscow as before. Diplomatic status gave them free access both departing Berlin and on arrival in Moscow.

Dmitri delivered the suitcase to Grigory immediately. The technical team began work on cracking the code and Dmitri went home.

His mobile phone ringing woke him from a deep sleep. It was Grigory.

'Good news, Dmitri! The suitcase wasn't full of New Yorker magazines.'

'That's good news.'

'Not really. It was filled with Stern magazines.'

'Shit.'

'Yes, shit, we've outlaid over $200,000 plus travel and accommodation for a heap of old magazines. I hope you like reading.'

'Grigory, I assure you I will get to the bottom of this. It must be the Fijian Captain Kabu. He's the prick who sold the bomb to TMA .'

'You better go and find him.'

Suva Fiji 2024

Colonel Raka had been Prime Minister for a little over twelve months. In that time, he had brought stability to the once unstable government of the Pacific Island nation.

He was reading a report his government had commissioned on climate change and the effect it was having on Fiji. He was very concerned with what he read. Fiji could be below the sea in less than thirty years.

This was a similar report to the one that Prime Minister Inoke had read which motivated him to form EDO and manufacture six atomic bombs.

Prime Minister Raka called together his two closest ministers, Temo Ovini and Francis Banuve.

'Gentlemen, I have just completed reading a report on global warming and it's very disturbing. I now think Prime Minister Inoke was correct in his actions. He forced the big polluters to significantly reduce their carbon emissions. Having said that the commitment seems to have waned since EDO ceased to exist.'

'What do you think we should do, sir?'

'It is my understanding there are four bombs left located in New York, Beijing, New Delhi and Berlin. I suggest we resurrect EDO using social media and start making demands.'

'Harry, we mustn't forget what happened to Inoke,' said Temo.

'I don't think his untimely death had anything to do with his activities with EDO. Inoke was a very wealthy man and the police believe it was a kidnapping gone wrong.'

'You're probably right.'

EDO Returns

Chapter 33

EDO has Returned
Sponsored

👍 Like Page

We were encouraged initially by the actions of the big polluters responding to our demands, however, since EDO has been quiet they have abandoned their environmental programs and reverted to their old filthy ways. EDO has no alternative but to reactivate the four atomic bombs in our possession if we don't see a significant change we will detonate the first bomb.

www.EDO.com
Save the World

TIME IS NOT ON OUR SIDE

Learn More

1.2M   50K Comments   1M Shares

👍 Like   💬 Comment   ➢ Share

Oval Office, White House
Washington DC

President Donald Cooper was now in his second term. He was pleased the way things were going. Inflation was at its lowest level for many years as was the unemployment rate. America's growth rate was 3.5% and the country was not involved in any wars.

He received a telephone call from his Secretary of State, William Morris.

'May I come and see you, Mr President? I have something extremely important to discuss with you.'

'Anything wrong, Bill?

'I'd rather discuss it with you face to face if you don't mind.'

'OK, come over now. I have a thirty-minute window before the French President arrives.'

The Secretary of State was driven the three miles from the Harry Truman Building where his department was located to the White House.

A Secret Service operative showed him into the Oval Office.

'Good morning Bill; take a seat. Can I get you anything?'

'No thank you, sir, I'm fine.'

'It's been a long time since you've called me *sir* in private, Bill. This meeting must be serious.'

'I'm afraid it is. The environmental terrorist group, EDO, has raised its ugly head again. They are threatening to detonate an atomic bomb in a major city if we don't meet their demands.'

'Fuck it. I thought we had heard the last of them.'

'We all did.'

'Do we know what their demands are?'

'Not yet.'

'Keep me posted and in the meantime I will direct the CIA and the FBI to dedicate a large proportion of their resources to finding these terrorists.'

'Thank you. Goodbye sir.'

'Goodbye, Bill.'

President Cooper welcomed the recently elected French President, Alfred Couture, to the office. Apart from trade and the Middle East, President Cooper raised the topic of EDO and the global threat they presented. Naturally, the French President was alarmed.

When M Couture left, Donald Cooper asked his private secretary to contact Beijing, Berlin, and New Delhi and arrange for a video conference.

Situation Room White House
The President had gathered his War Cabinet together.
Present were:
Vice President Graham Anderson
Secretary of State William Morris
Secretary of Defence Michelle Bennett
Secretary of Energy David Murphy
Secretary of the Treasury Ian Bryant

Moscow Russia War Room:
President Alexander Ivanov
Boris Smirnov Directorate KR: External Counter-Intelligence
Egor Kuznetsov Directorate OT: Operational and Technical Support
Feodore Popov Directorate R: Operational Planning and Analysis:
Gavrie Vasiliev Directorate I: Computer Service
Dusan Sokolov Directorate of Economic Intelligence

Other countries present were:
German Chancellor Helmut Wagner
President of India Arnav Bakshi
President of China Mrs Fei Hong Zhou
Prime Minister of Great Britain Geoffrey Baird
President of France Alfred Couture

'Ladies and Gentlemen we find ourselves once again in a precarious situation. This terrorist group calling themselves EDO are threatening us all with nuclear annihilation.

'Not one of our counter-terrorist organisations has been able to get close to identifying this group. We represent the most powerful nations in the world yet we are being held to ransom,' said President Cooper.

'What you say is true, President Cooper, but it does nothing to help us solve our dilemma,' said President Ivanov.

'Weren't there some leads taking us to Fiji?' asked Helmut Wagner.

'We did follow up on some leads but they led us nowhere. Fiji is the 150th largest country in the world. Eritrea is bigger. they don't have the resources to build sophisticated atomic bombs so it just doesn't make sense,' said President Cooper.

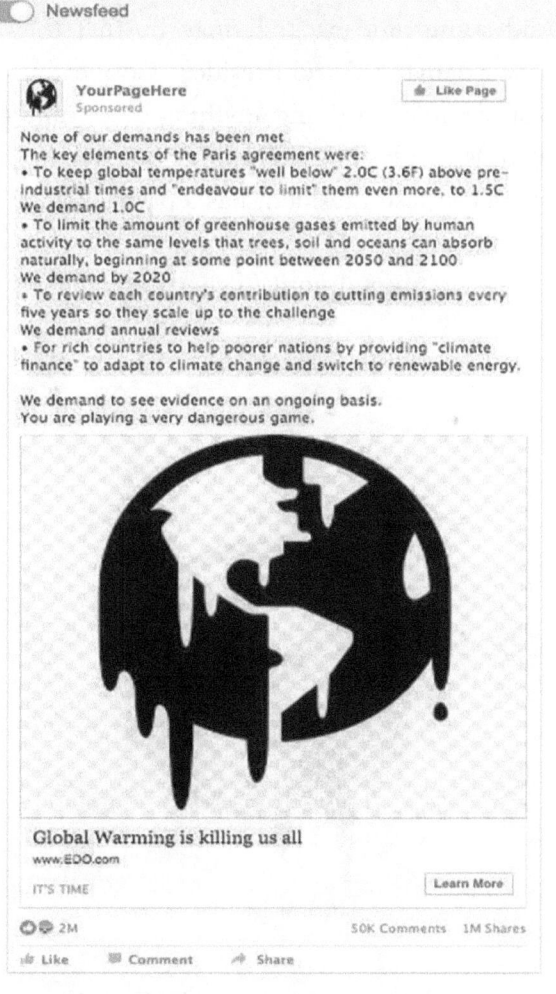

'So where does it leave us? asked the President of China.

'I think we have to wait to see what their latest demands are,' said President Cooper.

The video conference closed with an agreement they would get together again once EDO publicised their next demands.

'I didn't think the bastards would release their demands so soon. I suppose we better call another video conference.'

The video conference was arranged for the following week.

'As you are all aware, we have been reminded by EDO as to what the cornerstone of their demands are. They don't stipulate any specifics but we know they did some time back. It may be that they are becoming more flexible in their demands,' said President Cooper.

'May I suggest we hold off doing anything more until they do outline their specific demands,' said Mrs Fei Hong Zhou.

'Yes, I think the Chinese President has a point,' said Helmut Wagner, the German Chancellor.

The meeting was adjourned until further notice. They didn't have to wait long.

It was obvious EDO had become very active again and the major powers knew they had to act quickly and decisively.

Vory also knew they must uncover where in Fiji EDO were located.

Moscow

Grigory called in Dmitri to his office.

'It looks like our friends in Fiji are up to their old tricks again, Dmitri.'

'It would seem so, Grigory.'

'Do you think they have possession of the bombs?'

'They may well have, considering the bombs were stored in their embassies. Initially, anyway.'

'What do you think our chances would be taking them off their hands?'

'It wouldn't be easy considering they are a foreign government with an army protecting the Prime Minister and his cabinet.'

'How large is their military?'

'Not large, but very well trained.'

'Go away and come up with a plan. I want to see something from you within a month.'

'Yes, Grigory. I'll do my best.'

'It better be your best. I hold you responsible for the stuff-ups relating to the magazines in New York and Berlin.'

196

THE MISSION

CHAPTER 34

September 2024

Dmitri called Grigory's office to request a meeting with his boss. It was granted. The meeting would be on the following Thursday at 5pm.

Dmitri was convinced the plan he had contrived would work. If Grigory approved it they would need to act quickly.

Dmitri had been waiting in Grigory's waiting room for over thirty minutes which the senior Vory operative figured was a form of punishment.

At last, the receptionist advised him to go into the Mafia boss's office.

'Good afternoon, Dmitri. Your message indicated you have a plan to recover the bombs. So let's hear it.'

Dmitri outlined his proposal.

Grigory was impressed.

'You're sure you can pull it off?'

'I'm very sure, Grigory. I would bet my life on it.'

'You probably will be.'

'I understand, sir. I will need the necessary resources as quickly as possible; time is of the essence.'

'Let me know what you need and I'll make sure you get everything you that you require.'

'Thank you, Grigory. I won't let you down.'

'No, you won't.'

Dmitri, Dannill, Alexey, and Sergey arranged for flights to Suva and once they arrived, Dmitri arranged to meet a Vory operative who was stationed in Fiji.

His name was Igor Pavlov. Grigory had organised the equipment required for the operation to be delivered to Igor's house. The two Vory men loaded the equipment into the VW Kombi van. On his way back to the hotel, Dmitri stopped to buy a copy of the Fiji Times. The headline news related to the Prime Minister, Colonel Raka, who would be undergoing surgery for an enlarged prostate. It was anticipated it would be a straightforward procedure

The surgeon who would operate on the Prime Minister was Dr Bhandari, Fiji's most respected surgeon.

He lived in Suva's most prestigious suburbs Domain/Muanikau with his wife Anika and their three children; fifteen-year-old Argan, and the thirteen-year-old twins, Kabir and Jenya.

The family was eating dinner together; the children's favourite dish of fish and chips with salad on the side.

The talk at the table revolved around the operation Dr Bhandari was to perform the following day. It wasn't because it was a prostate. He had performed hundreds of similar operations. It was because it was the Prime Minister who would be relying on the surgeon's skill.

The front doorbell rang and Argan went to answer it. He returned with four men in balaclavas holding Glock pistols with silencers.

Glock Pistol

'Everybody stand up behind your chair.

Two of the men tied their wrists behind their backs with nylon ties. They then inserted a cloth gag to stop them from making any noise.

'OK, sit on the sofa, except for the good doctor. You come with me, sir.'

Two of the men marched Dr Bhandari to the main bedroom.

'Doctor I'm going the remove the gag. If you yell or scream I'll shoot you. Do you understand?'

The doctor nodded. One of the men untied the gag.

'Do you love your wife, Doctor?'

'Of course I do.'

'Do you love your children?'

'Very much so.'

'That's good. If you want your family to live you have to do what I ask you to do.'

Beads of sweat ran down the surgeon's face. 'You touch my family and I'll…'

'You'll do what? We've got the guns, not you.'

'What do you want me to do?'

'That's the idea, doc.'

The other man who hadn't said anything spoke up.

'You will be operating on the Prime Minister tomorrow. We want you to take this capsule and squeeze the liquid into his bloodstream. He will go into a seizure and die. The liquid is untraceable; it will just look like an unfortunate operating room incident.'

'What's in the capsule?'

'Best you not know. I can tell you it's not Aspro.'

'You can't ask me to kill the Prime Minister. I'm trained to save lives, not take them.'

'Right, well you'd better go into the living room and say goodbye to your family.'

'Hold on, why are you doing this? By the sound of your accent, you are Eastern European. Why do you want our Prime Minister dead?'

'We have our reasons and it's not your business. Are you going to cooperate or are you all going to die?'

'I suppose I don't have a choice.'

'Good, we have a few ground rules. My phone will show any calls you make on the way or in the hospital so don't try and be smart.

My iPad is connected to all the CCTVs on the route, including your dash cam and in the hospital. We will be watching your every move including inside the operating theatre. Is that understood?'

'Yes, I understand.'

'Go and join your family. Wait, I need to gag you again.'

'Is that absolutely necessary?'

'We don't want you to communicate with each other.'

'Remove the gags, Alexey they've served their purpose,' said Dmitri.

Suva September 23

Government House Suva

Temo Ovini, Defence Minister, and Francis Banuve, Treasurer, were visiting their good friend and colleague Prime Minister Raka at Government House, the Prime Minister's official residence.

'Are you feeling nervous, Harry?'

'No, not really. It's not open-heart surgery. Besides, I have Dr Bhandari who's regarded as the best in Fiji.'

'I suppose you will have a private room,' said Francis in jest.

'I sincerely hope so.'

'When do you get admitted, Harry?' asked Temo.

'I believe it's 10am tomorrow.'

'How long will you be in for?'

'They have told me seven days,'

'That's not long for me to be acting Prime Minister,' said Temo.

'Sorry, it's the best I could do, Temo.'

The three good friends laughed.

Mrs Raka entered the room.

'I'm afraid I've must ask you to leave now as the Prime Minister needs to rest. He has a big day tomorrow.'

'We'll visit you Harry; take care,' said Temo.

The two men left the Prime Minister to have a nap.

Dmitri bribed two ambulance drivers to not only take the Prime Minister to hospital but to take the dead Prime Minister away from the operating room immediately with the excuse he required a post mortem at the morgue as soon as possible so a press statement could be released.

September 24

Dr Bhandari was given his instructions: there would no stopping on the way and he was to act normally when he arrived at the hospital. He would scrub down and chat with the nurses as he normally did.

The ambulance pulled up under the magnificent portico and waited for their Very Important Patient. Two Government House employees helped the Prime Minister out to the ambulance. They began the twenty-minute journey to the CWH Hospital.

CWS Hospital

The ambulance arrived on time and the gurney was lowered down and wheeled into the hospital. The ambulance officers waited for the lift to take them to the sixth floor where the operating theatres were located.

The Prime Minister was wheeled into operating theatre 4 where he was transferred to the operating table. There was eight medical staff in the room including the theatre nurses the anaesthetist plus Dr Bhandari.

'Wow, all these people just for me.'

'You're a very special patient, Prime Minister,' said Dr Bhandari. 'You understand why you're here, sir?'

'Yes, I'm having my prostate removed.'

'Prime Minister I will be injecting a drug called Propofol which will make you relaxed,' said Jack Rabuka, the anaesthetist. 'I will then administer anaesthesia. You'll wake up a new man.'

'I certainly hope so. I'll see you all in a few hours.'

'You probably won't, sir. You'll be waking up in your hospital room.'

The Propofol was injected and it wasn't long before the patient was feeling a little woozy. Jack then fed the anaesthesia into his arm and ten seconds later the Prime Minister was out to it.

Dr Bhandari made an incision in the lower part of his abdomen. Three hours, later the prostate had been removed plus several lymph nodes in case cancer was present. They were about to close the Prime Minister up when an alarm began to sound.

'Doctor, his blood pressure has dropped to a dangerous level,' said the head theatre nurse.

'What's happening with the ECG?'

'His heartbeat is forty.'

'Give me the defibrillator pads, nurse.'

Dr Bhandari used the shock treatment on his patient, knowing it was useless. After thirty minutes of trying to revive the Prime Minister, he proclaimed the patient dead. Dr Bhandari closed up the paitent.

Dr Bhandari called for the ambulance officers to take him to the morgue where a post mortem would be conducted. Dr Bhandari had been instructed by his captors to accompany the PM in the ambulance.

Once the deceased Prime Minister was placed in the ambulance, Dr Bhandari joined him and the vehicle raced off to its destination. The siren was silent.

'Doctor, I have been instructed to give you this needle. You must inject it in the Prime Minister's chest immediately.'

'Why? He's dead.'

'I have my instructions and you have yours.'

The doctor injected the large needle and within fifteen minutes the PM was breathing again. Dr Bhandari checked all his vital signs and they were close to being normal.

The doctor was astounded as he had never seen anything like this before in his long career.

The ambulance entered a long bitumen driveway lined with beautiful trees. The house was colonial in design with verandas and French doors.

The ambulance officers lifted the gurney onto the driveway and took it into the house. Waiting for them was a man in a balaclava. It was Dmitri.

'Welcome to my humble abode, Prime Minister. You are to be my guest for a little while.'

Dmitri directed the ambos to a large bedroom at the rear of the house. They placed him in a queen-sized bed.

'I suggest you rest, sir, as you have a busy day ahead tomorrow.'

Dmitri left the room, locking it behind him. He ran straight into Dr Bhandari.

'Ah doctor, I've been looking for you.'

'I've been looking for you also. I completed my side of the deal. When will you let my family go?'

'They have already been released, doctor. Go home. I'll arrange for a car to drive you.'

'Is that it?'

'Yes, doctor, that is it.'

Dmitri was true to his word. He arranged a car and driver to take the good doctor home.

Dr Bhandari was dropped off outside his home. He unlocked the front door and walked in. His wife and children were huddled on the couch, fearing it was the terrorist returning to kill them all. When they saw who it was they all jumped up hugging Bhandari and crying.

The family would never be the same again.

THE INTERROGATION

CHAPTER 35

The Prime Minister slept well, which was understandable considering what he had been through. When he woke, he began to realise he was in a precarious position. Why was he being kept prisoner and what did these men want?

A man in a balaclava unlocked the door and brought in a bowl of cereal, two slices of toast and a mug of coffee.

'I'm not hungry.'

'I suggest you eat it. You're going to need all your strength.'

'What do you want with me?'

'You'll find out soon enough. Now eat your fucking breakfast.'

He left the room, locking it behind him.

'What sort of space is he in?' asked Dmitri.

'He's pretty defiant at this stage,' answered Alexey.

'That's to be expected. He'll cooperate after a little persuasion.'

'When do you intend to begin the interrogation?'

'Tomorrow. I want him to wonder what's going to happen to him plus we need him reasonably fit.'

The following morning after another delicious breakfast, three masked men entered the PM's bedroom.

'Good morning Harry. You don't mind if we call you Harry, do you?'

'I don't care what you call me. Just tell me what's going on.'

'Tell me, Harry, what do you remember of the last few days?'

'I remember being wheeled into an operating theatre to have my prostate removed. The next thing I know I'm being held captive by you.'

'That's pretty well it. We might fill in the details for you later on. The reason why you're here is to tell us where the four atomic bombs are located.'

'I've got no idea what you're talking about.'

'That's what your predecessor Inoke said before we convinced him otherwise.'

'So, it was you who murdered him.'

'We like to think he passed away during questioning.'

'I don't know where these bombs are located.'

'Are you the head of EDO?'

'No, that was Inoke.'

'We know you resurrected EDO after Inoke passed away.'

'That's not true.'

'I think we should introduce you to the elephant. Inoke didn't enjoy the introduction much.'

'I was a colonel in the army. I think you'll find I'm not easy to break.'

'We'll see. Put your hands behind your back.'

The Prime Minister complied and he was handcuffed. The gas mask was fitted over his face. The questioning began with the hose being squeezed for up to one and a half minutes.

After two sessions, the Prime Minister had vomited in the mask and was close to death, but he refused to divulge where the bombs were located.

'OK, that's enough. Lay him down on his bed and let him rest. We'll try again tomorrow,' said Dmitri.

The Prime Minister endured a fitful sleep as he knew he would have to endure the elephant again.

The masked man unlocked the Prime Minister's door, bringing him his breakfast.

'Are you hungry this morning?'

'Yes, I'm famished.'

'I thought you might be. You didn't eat dinner last night.'

'What have you brought me?'

'I'm afraid it's the same old.'

'Never mind.'

The other two masked men came into the room soon afterwards. One was carrying the gas mask.

'Good morning, Harry. Are you willing to cooperate with us today or is it the elephant again?'

'All I know is what I read in Inoke's files he had locked away in his safe. There were four atomic bombs stored in storerooms in our embassies in New York, New Delhi, Berlin, and Beijing, As far as I know, they are still there. I resurrected EDO for the same reason that Inoke created it. We were both worried that Fiji would be submerged without significant action by the major polluters of the world. That's all I know.'

'So you believe the bombs are in your embassies?'

'Yes, I assume so.'

'For your information, the bombs in New York and Berlin were taken out.'

'What do you mean, taken out?'

'They were swapped for dummies, suitcases with old magazines.'

'Do you know if the other two are still in the embassies?' asked Harry.

'We don't know yet.'

'I can assure you I had no idea they were swapped.'

The three Mafioso left the room, locking the door behind them.

'I don't think he knows anything about the nukes. He's speaking the truth,' said Dmitri.

'What should we do with him?' said Alexey.

'I'm going to drop him off near Government House. There's no need to execute him. It would only cause an international incident.'

'What should we do?'

'Wait here for me to return, then we'll fly out of here.'

Dmitri loaded the Prime Minister into the Range Rover. He blindfolded him and insisted he lie down in the back seat. The trip only took twenty minutes.

'OK, Harry. I'm going to take your blindfold off. You are only five minutes from your home. Goodbye.'

The Prime Mister began walking to Government House. He couldn't believe his luck.

Dmitri drove to the airport and purchased a ticket to Tahiti. This was where he anticipated he would live for the rest of his life. He had no desire to face Grigory. His intention was to bring his wife and children over to join him as soon as it was safe to do so.

APOCALYPSE

CHAPTER 36

The commodore feared Kabu was lost at sea, having failed to return to the Bodrum Sailing Club after a period of three weeks. He issued a decree for all capable craft to search for their valued member and his yacht *Dragonfly*.

Eventually, the search was abandoned. The conclusion was Kabu had encountered a fierce storm and sunk.

Unbeknownst to the searchers, Kabu's plan was to sail to Greece where he would change the name of his yacht to *Amatae et Amissae*. The translation from Latin meant "Loved and Lost", a tribute to his late wife Mila and his lover Esma. His intention was to moor the yacht indefinitely.

He changed his name to Christian Hoover and now with both he and his yacht incognito, he hoped he would go unrecognised.

Halfway through his journey he actually did encounter a fierce storm.

He woke at three am having been thrown from his bunk. The yacht was pitching heavily. He looked at the radar. The storm was rated at 11 and the winds were gusting over 100 kilometres an hour. He turned on his laptop computer.

A dangerous windstorm with storm force winds and major waves in the Aegean region is current

He climbed up onto the deck and took the wheel. The sky above was filled with lightning and the sound of the thunder was frightening. Kabu fought the seas for the next few hours. The waves were towering over the yacht's mast.

The storm dissipated by mid-morning. The lone yachtsman was exhausted. He turned on the autopilot and slept until three in the afternoon.

When Kabu woke, he checked the yacht's navigation system. Apparently *Amatae et Amissae* would arrive at its destination within eight hours.

The yacht sailed into Piraeus Sailing Club just before midnight.

Kabu's intention was to lease a berth for the next twelve months, knowing full well the yacht would never be sailed by him again. Next morning, Kabu approached the sailing club manager.

'Hello, my name is Christian Hoover. I would like to lease a berth if I could.'

'Yes, we have a berth available. How long would you like lease it for?'

'Twelve months if that's OK.'

'Yes, we can accommodate you. The fee is 30,000 drachmas per month.'

Christian did a quick calculation and it worked out just below $100 US.

Piraeus sailing Club

Christian aka Kabu stayed at the sailing club for the following week, and then took a train to Sofia in Bulgaria. He rented a short-term furnished apartment.

Kabu needed to decide what his next step would be. His intention was to immigrate to a country similar to Fiji. He missed the clear blue water and white sandy beaches. His research brought him to the conclusion that Hawaii would be the ideal destination; preferably Maui.

Kabu began researching the island and suitable real estate. He discovered a house which seemed to be ideal. It was priced at $10,000,000, which was within his budget.

He knew he needed to submit his application for citizenship before he could purchase the villa.

Kabu decided to get the wheels turning by making a visit to the US Embassy.

U S Embassy Sofia

The Fijian national approached the young woman behind the bulletproof glass. She used a microphone to inquire about the purpose of his visit.

'I wish to immigrate to America.'

'What is your current nationality?'

'English.'

'Who will be sponsoring you?'

'What do you mean?'

'A foreign citizen must be sponsored by a U.S. citizen unless you have a relative with permanent residency. If you are intending to work in the United States, your employer could sponsor you.'

'No, I don't intend to work and I don't have a sponsor.'

'Then I'm sorry, I can't help you.'

'Forget it. I'll stay in Bulgaria.'

'I'm sorry sir, but they are the rules.'

Kabu walked out of the embassy building feeling very dejected.

The words on the plaque attached to the Statue of Liberty were obviously bullshit.

Give me your tired, your poor, Your huddled masses yearning to breathe free, The wretched refuse of your teeming shore. Send these, the homeless; tempest-tossed to me, I lift my lamp beside the golden door!

Kabu returned to his townhouse and began to brood. This developed into depression, the Black Dog, as Winston Churchill called this affliction.

All he wanted was a quiet life in Hawaii and to try and forget what had happened in his life over the past few years.

He didn't eat much but he began to drink again and his mood became even darker. He ensured there was minimal light entering the house. He had entered a state of deep depression in which he suffered panic attacks as he felt the entire world was against him.

Kabu's sleep patterns became erratic. Some nights he didn't sleep at all. He just lay in his bed conjuring up plans as to how he could pay America back for rejecting him. His mental ill-health wasn't just triggered by his rejection; it all went back to the enormous guilt he felt re Tel Aviv and Tehran. After all, he was ultimately responsible for millions losing their lives.

Kabu applied for a tourist visa enabling him to stay in America for three months. He flew business class to New York and rented an apartment in Manhattan. He had visited New York several times before and always enjoyed it, but despite staying in one of his favourite cities he remained in his apartment feeling as black as ever.

After a week of solitude, he devised a plan which, if successful, would even the score with the USA.

He rented a Ford Mustang and drove to Queens. He parked in front of the New York Storage Facility Company where he had rented a storage garage some time ago. He opened the storage unit and took out one of four suitcases stored there. He placed it in the trunk of the Ford and drove off.

Kabu's next stop was New York Boat Rentals where he rented a top of the range speedboat with two 90 horsepower motors on the back.

Alan and Patricia Lucas plus their two children Michael, seventeen, and Rebecca, sixteen, were nearing the end of their holiday in the USA. They lived in Hobart, Tasmania and they were all visiting America for the first time. The holiday began in Los Angeles where they spent a day at Disneyland. Naturally, Pirates of the Caribbean was the favourite as Michael and Rebecca had seen all the films.

The following day the family took the Universal Studios tour in the morning and walked the Walk of Fame in the afternoon.

Alan wanted to travel to San Francisco for two reasons. He was keen to visit Haight Ashbury, home of the hippies in the sixties, and Alcatraz, the home of Al Capone.

Patricia and the two children weren't keen but they did want to visit San Francisco. As it turned out, they enjoyed the tour of Alcatraz and were intrigued by the history of Haight Ashbury.

'So dad was that film with Clint Eastwood true?' asked Michael.

'It was, three men escaped. As a result they closed the prison.'

'Did they ever find them?'

'No, they still don't know if they lived or died?' said Alan.

'I think most people hoped they lived.'

'Yeah, they deserved to get away.' said Michael.

215

The next and final destination for the Lucas family was New York from where they would fly to London to begin their European tour.

The Delta 777 landed at JFK Airport in the late afternoon. The family checked into the Novatel Hotel, showered and went down to the restaurant for dinner.

'So what's the plan for tomorrow, Mum?' asked Rebecca.

'Well, seeing we are in New York, I think we should ride up to the top of the Empire State building in the morning. I'm sure the view would be stunning.'

'That sounds great; then what?'

'I suggest we catch the ferry to Liberty Island and climb the Statue of Liberty. That would be a very New York thing to do.'

'How many steps, Mum?' asked Michael.

'Lots, about three-hundred-and-fifty, I believe.'

'So, is everybody up for it?' asked Patricia.

'Yeah, let's do it,' said Alan.

The Lucas family rode the fast lift up to the top of the iconic building. The reports were accurate; the 360-degree views were stunning.

They rode down just as fast and had lunch in the famous State Grill and Bar.

The next stop was Liberty Island Ferry, which took twenty minutes to reach the monument.

'Wow, I can't believe how big it is,' said Michael.

'It's huge,' said Rebecca.

'Are you still up for the climb?' said Alan.

'Yep, let's do it.'

The four Australian tourists began the long climb.

'My God, it seems like we are climbing forever,' said Rebecca.

'Come on Becky, it's only about another one-hundred-and-fifty steps to go,' said Michael.

'That's great, thanks, Michael.'

The family finally reached the crown, with its windows looking out over New York Bay and New York City.

They enjoyed their well-earned rest looking out of the crown's windows.

It was Michael who first noticed the fast-approaching launch.

'Hey, Dad, I read that private boats are prohibited from getting close to the island. That boat is heading straight for us.'

'I think you're right, son. I wonder what's he's up to.'

Stuart Hardwick was thirty-five years old. He was a very successful stockbroker with Cohen & Co on Wall Street. He was born in Denver, Colorado, where his parents owned an accounting practice. Stuart went to Harvard University where he studied business.

Grace Smith was a thirty-year-old lawyer with Outten & Golden who specialised in business law.

They met through mutual friends and soon became an item. After two years of dating, they moved in together, living in Brooklyn.

'Grace, can I entice you to join me for lunch today?'

'That would be lovely, Stuart. Any special reason?'

'No, it's such a beautiful day I thought eating at Battery Park on the water would be great. I always enjoy the view of the Bay while eating a lobster.'

Battery Park Restaurant

'I'll meet you there. What time?'

'Let's say 12.30.'

'Awesome. See you then.'

Stuart was already sitting at the table overlooking New York Bay when the love of his life arrived. He had ordered a bottle of Verve Clique.

'Champagne! What's the occasion?'

Stuart removed a small box from his suit pocket, opened it and showed the contents to Grace. It was a one-carat diamond ring.

'Will you marry me, Grace?'

'Yes, of course, I will. Oh my God.'

The waiter poured the newly engaged couple champagne. They lifted their glasses and raised a toast to the rest of their lives together.

It was a beautiful day with not a cloud in the sky and the water was calm. Kabu was heading for Liberty Island. He knew private boats were prohibited from getting closer than 1000 feet from the Statue of Liberty but that didn't worry him.

Kabu sped in close to the island. He then cut the engines. He knew the water police would be alongside his boat any minute and he therefore needed to make a decision. He picked up the detonation device. He kept looking at the monument and all the people walking around Liberty Island.

He placed the detonator on the passenger seat and started the engines. He then caught sight of two police boats heading his way. He picked up the deadly device, shut his eyes and pressed the button.

The Statue of Liberty melted into a slagheap on the blackened earth. The 5000 visitors on what was Liberty Island were vaporised, including the Lucas family.

The mushroom cloud rose above the Upper New York Bay then spread across the bay, hitting Manhattan and Brooklyn. Stuart and Grace heard the boom and witnessed the mushroom cloud rising above the harbour and what was Liberty Island. Before they could react, a nuclear windstorm smashed them against the restaurant wall and soon after they were enveloped in fire. Their wish to live the rest of their lives together came true.

Liberty Island is located 3.28 kilometres from New York. That distance restricted the death rate to 1,000,000 it could easily have been 8,000,000.

The Aftermath

Chapter 37

The people of New York were going about their business. The majority of the population in the central business district of Manhattan were employed in one of the city's notorious skyscrapers.

When the bomb exploded, those closest to the bay had their windows shattered, giving them little protection from radiation fallout. Those farther away remained safe.

Sirens were howling from both fire trucks and police cars. The police had been instructed by headquarters to use their loud hailers to notify the population to remain inside their buildings to avoid nuclear fallout.

Some police were selected to wear white protective overalls and approach the bay area where most of the damage had been done. As they approached the area, they discovered charred and mangled bodies in the street, unrecognizable as human beings.

Several police launches approached what remained of Liberty Island. The monument had literally melted into the bay. There was no sign of human remains as the tourists on the island at the time of the explosion were vaporised. Their shadows would be discovered when it became safe to step onto the island.

White House Washington

President Donald Cooper was in the situation room in the White House. With him were:

Vice President Graham Anderson

Secretary of State William Morris

Secretary of Defence Michelle Bennett

Secretary of Energy David Murphy

Secretary of the Treasury Ian Bryant

'What in the fuck is going on here? There hasn't been an atomic bomb exploded in anger since Hiroshima and Nagasaki and now within twelve months we have three bombs detonated in three major cities. Who do we think it was?'

'We believe it was TMA again. They've already proved they have the capability by blowing up Tel Aviv,' said the Secretary of Defence.

'Who's *we*?'

'The CIA and the Defence Department.'

'Why isn't Lewis Pentecost here? He's head of the CIA.'

'He wasn't called to be here, Mr President,' said Graham Anderson.

'TMA is his baby, so better get him here now.'

Graham Anderson excused himself from the meeting and made a call to his old friend Lewis.

'Hello, Lewis, the President would like to see you in the situation room immediately.'

'I should have been included in the fucking meeting in the first place.'

'I know you should have. It was simply an oversight. Now get over to the White House immediately.'

'OK, I'll be there as soon as I can.'

'Good. I'll see you soon.'

The Vice President returned to the meeting, confirming the head of the CIA was on his way.

Ten minutes later, Lewis Pentecost was led into the situation room, ironically, by a CIA operative.

'Hello, Lewis, take a seat and brief us all about what you know about this bomb.'

'Mr President, as you know, it's early days. After all this all only happened yesterday.'

'Yes, but no doubt it's been planned for quite some time. Why wasn't the CIA on top of what was being planned? Isn't that your fucking job?'

'Please forgive me, Mr President, but it is very difficult to infiltrate groups such as TMA.'

'So, you believe it was TMA who committed this atrocity?'

221

'That would be our best guess.'

'Lewis, I'm not interested in your fucking guessing. Go away and find out who blew up half of New York.

'OK, ladies and gentlemen, let's call it quits for now. We'll reconvene when more information comes to light.'

The President returned to the Oval Office where he requested a cup of tea and his favourite muffin; blueberry. He'd just taken a sip of his tea when his secretary announced the President of Russia, Alexander Ivanov, was on the telephone.

'Good afternoon, Alexander. I take it you are calling about the disaster in New York?'

'I am; my condolences, Donald. Do you have any idea who committed this atrocity?'

'We have our suspicions but no solid proof yet.'

'Do you intend to ask the Secretary General to call a Security Council meeting?'

'Not yet. We would like some more intelligence to bring to the council.'

'Donald, if there is anything Russia can do please let us know.'

'Thank you for your support, Alexander.'

'It goes without saying, Donald. Goodbye.'

'Goodbye.'

Over the next few days, the President received calls from many world leaders from Britain to Fiji.

As was their modus operandi, TMA claimed responsibility for the atrocity. The United States believed them, as did the rest of the world.

An alliance was formed, including the USA, Russia, Britain, Germany, France and many more nations. Their mandate was to destroy this evil group once and for all. After twelve months of intensive fighting, TMA was declared dead.

Kabu went to his maker without the stain of mass murderer against his name.

The End

EPILOGUE

EDO may have been responsible for the death of over one million innocent lives however they achieved significant gains in controlling climate change.

China

Cancelled 106 coal powered power stations, which had been approved for construction. Replaced them with wind and solar farms.

Ceased building 130 coal-powered power stations.

Decommissioned four hundred coal-powered power stations, replacing them with clean energy alternatives.

India

Cancelled approval for 66 coal-powered power stations, replacing them with clean alternatives.

Ceased construction of forty-one coal fired stations.

Decommissioned existing power stations by 120.

USA

Decommissioned 130 coal-powered stations

Germany

Decommissioned thirty five coal-powered stations

Replace with solar and wind power.

Russia

Ceased construction of ten coal fired stations.

Decommissioned thirty coal-powered stations.

Replace with solar and wind power.

Electric cars were widely adopted by many countries largely to do with EDO's influence.

BP's board, chaired by Sir Humphrey Harmsworth, were fired at a shareholders meeting having been outed by EDO.

BP reverted to investing in green energy £800,000 was invested in the first year.

Other international companies followed suit.

Prime Minister Raka returned to office after one month of recuperating from his prostate operation. General elections were held a year later. Raka was elected for a further three years and re-elected for a further term after that. Stability in Fiji became the norm.

Bibliography

𝓏   WRECKSITE - WILLIAM K. VANDERBILT CARGO SHIP 1942-1943   https://www.wrecksite.eu/wreck

𝓋   William Kissam Vanderbilt - Wikipedia

𝓋   Marine salvage - Wikipedia

𝓏   Would a Boeing 737, converted to use as a bomber, be virtually unstoppable in WWII? - Quora

𝓋   Argo (ROV) - Wikipedia

𝄞   RH3 Yacht Charter Details, Explorer yacht | CHARTERWORLD Luxury Superyachts

𝓋   Nuclear weapon design - Wikipedia

𝄞   Duncan Clark on the carbon footprint of nuclear war | Environment | The Guardian

𝄞   The Pacific Islands - Cop23

𝓏   What is the smallest sized atomic bomb that can be made? - Quora

𝓋   FijiOMCmap - Geography of Fiji - Wikipedia

☷   Most EU countries set to miss 2020 carbon emission reduction targets: report

𝄞   5 successful treasure hunters you've probably never heard of - Escapes in Time

𝄞   8 Nuclear Weapons the U.S. Has Lost | Mental Floss

𝓋   USS Ticonderoga (CV-14) - Wikipedia

𝓋   Naval Station Newport - Wikipedia

𝄞   AK-101 Mod.1 | Pimp My Gun Wiki | FANDOM powered by Wikia

𝄞   Incredible Technology: Salvaging Shipwrecks

𝓏   What is the chain of command on a aircraft carrier? - Quora

𝓋   B43 nuclear bomb - Wikipedia

𝓋   List of countries by carbon dioxide emissions - Wikipedia

    Bila Gun Battery - Fiji Museum

225

To reduce greenhouse gases from cows and sheep, we need to look at the big picture

Reducing livestock greenhouse gas emissions | Agriculture and Food

Study: Meat And Dairy Produce More Greenhouse Gases Than You Think

EV Global Warming Emissions and Fuel-Cost Savings (2012)

Cessna 208 Caravan - Wikipedia

14 Ways the Oil & Gas Industry is Becoming More Sustainable » Castagra

Opportunities for Drones to be Used by Helicopter Companies - Commercial UAV News

1 megatone nuclear bomb how far away is safe - Google Search

The effects of a single terrorist nuclear bomb - Bulletin of the Atomic Scientists

BP dropped green energy projects worth billions to focus on fossil fuels | Environment | The Guardian   https

What's put the spark in Norway's electric car revolution? | Money | The Guardian

Top 10 countries selling electric cars | AA Cars

Nuclear war between Israel and Iran: lethality beyond the pale

What Would Happen if Israel Nuked Iran – Mother Jones

THE EFFECTS OF A NUCLEAR BOMB EXPLOSION ON A CITY on JSTOR

THE EFFECTS OF A NUCLEAR BOMB EXPLOSION ON A CITY on JSTOR

NAE Website - A Nuclear Explosion in a City or an Attack on a Nuclear Reactor

Israel Defense Forces - Wikipedia

Politics of Iran - Wikipedia

Ayatollah Ali Khamenei controls £60 billion financial empire, report says - Telegraph

Middle East - Google Maps

What's put the spark in Norway's electric car revolution? | Money | The Guardian

Top 10 countries selling electric cars | AA Cars

Nuclear war between Israel and Iran: lethality beyond the pale

What Would Happen if Israel Nuked Iran – Mother Jones

THE EFFECTS OF A NUCLEAR BOMB EXPLOSION ON A CITY on JSTOR

THE EFFECTS OF A NUCLEAR BOMB EXPLOSION ON A CITY on JSTOR

NAE Website - A Nuclear Explosion in a City or an Attack on a Nuclear Reactor

Israel Defense Forces - Wikipedia

Politics of Iran - Wikipedia

Ayatollah Ali Khamenei controls £60 billion financial empire, report says - Telegraph

Middle East - Google Maps

Scenario: Middle East War | Future | FANDOM powered by Wikia

Next Middle East War Is Most Likely to Start In These Places, According to New Report

US naval presence off Syria sends clear signal | Financial Times

The Middle East Friendship Chart

Israel Defense Forces ranks - Wikipedia

Russian mafia - Wikipedia

The rise of the vory, Russia's 'super mafia' - RN - ABC News (Australian Broadcasting Corporation)

Fiji Embassy of Washington, D.C. - Embassy Staff - Akuila Vuira

Leadership — Central Intelligence Agency

Private Island Resort Fiji - Matangi Island

100 Most Common English Last Names

United States National Security Council - Wikipedia

Climate Change Problems For The Fiji Islands

Crimes involving radioactive substances - Wikipedia

Foreign Intelligence Service (Russia) - Wikipedia

Mapped: The world's coal power plants | Carbon Brief

Home | Carbon Brief » Clear on climate

The world is going slow on coal, but misinformation is distorting the facts | Environment | The Guardian

As Beijing Joins Climate Fight, Chinese Companies Build Coal Plants - The New York Times

Global Coal Plant Tracker | End Coal

Coal Plants by Country (Stations) - Google Sheets

Just 100 companies responsible for 71% of global emissions, study says | Guardian Sustainable Business | The Guardian

First published 2019 by Crabtree Pty Ltd

Global Warming is a work of fiction. Any resemblance to real persons, living or dead, is purely coincidental.

ISBN: 978-0-6484869-2-3 (p/b)

ISBN: 978-0-6484869-3-0 (ebook)

www.ingramcontent.com/pod-product-compliance
Lightning Source LLC
Chambersburg PA
CBHW050520260626
47157CB00004B/1403